LIBRARY AND ARCHIVES CANADA CATALOGUING IN PUBLICATION

Miles, Victoria, 1966-
     Mimi Power and the I-don't-know-what / by Victoria
Miles ; with illustrations by Marc Mongeau.

ISBN 978-1-896580-65-4

     I. Mongeau, Marc II. Title.

PS8576.I3235M54 2012   jC813'.54   C2012-902151-2

Book design by Elisa Gutiérrez

10 9 8 7 6 5 4 3 2 1

Printed and bound in Canada on FSC paper.

The publisher thanks the Government of Canada and Cana-
dian Heritage for their financial support through the
Canada Council for the Arts, the Canada Book Fund and
Livres Canada Books. The publisher also thanks the Government of the Province of British Columbia for the financial
support it has given through the Book Publishing Tax Credit
program and the British Columbia Arts Council.

VICTORIA MILES

Mimi Power
and the I-don't-know-what

illustrations by

MARC
MONGEAU

TRADEWIND BOOKS

Vancouver • London

In loving memory of Cyndi P.,
firm believer that
"We can't all go crazy at once,
we have to take turns."

Contents

PROLOGUE

It's very hard to tell your own story when you have a little sister barging in on it all the time, throwing your notebook in the air and losing your place.

Even if you find your pen again, it's hard to deal with the constant interruptions.

It's very hard, but it's not impossible.

CHAPTER ONE

Vitamin Orange

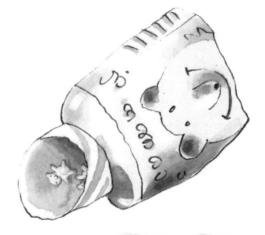

"Not that one!"

Here we go.

"Not the red one!"

This is a good place to start.

"No! That's squished! Not the squished one!"

We go through this every morning.

"That's red! I don't like red ones! No red 'tuff! I wan' onge!"

That's my sister. Lily June Power. Except nobody calls her that. At least nobody in my family does. What do we call her? Just wait, it takes some explaining. We'd better get through the vitamin thing first or we'll be on this page all day.

My mum is fishing around in a bottle of gummy bear vitamins, trying to find an orange one. She's starting to look a little desperate. I already got mine. I think it was green, but even if it were red, I wouldn't freak out about it. I'm nine. Nine-year-olds have bigger things going on.

For starters, today's bigger thing will be whether or not I have to get a late slip at school because my three-year-old sister is having a spaz. I already have six late slips this year because of Lily June. Now when I go to the office, Mrs. Peale, the secretary, just says, "Spaz again?" and hands me a slip. I think she makes them up early just for me. I'll bet she has one ready for today.

"Mimi, can you see an orange one in there?" Mum asks. She looks worried.

I peer into the bottle and shake it around a bit. "I don't think so, Mum. I think we got the last one yesterday."

"I wan' ONGE! ONGE!"

"How about this pretty little yellow one?" my mum coaxes.

"No LALLO! Onge!"

"Green?" squeaks Mum. "Green is nice!"

"No geen! ONGE!"

"Listen, Waby," says my mum, taking in a deep breath and trying to sound patient. "There aren't any orange. There just aren't any. Can't you pick a different colour?"

That's right. We call her Waby. It's a long story. I'll tell you later. Right now, back to the hollering. It starts like a faraway fire engine siren and gets louder, until you want to plug your ears and run from the room.

Mum starts grumbling about how, when she was a kid, there were no gummy bear vitamins, and the only vitamins she got tasted like chalk. She shakes the bottle and spills all the gummies onto the counter. Then she quickly sorts through them and gasps with relief.

"Look! I found one! Look, Waby! Here you go!"

Waby unscrunches her face and studies the gummy bear. For a second I think we're okay.

Maybe I'll make it to school on time after all. Waby reaches out and takes the vitamin. We're almost home free. She even has her mouth open, and she's not screaming. That's when she spots it.

And it's *not* okay.

"Not THAT one. THAT'S A SQUISHED ONE! NO SQUISHED ONE!"

One of the ears is mashed down. Plus, its head is a bit crooked. It is not perfect. Which means it is not good enough for my little sister. She's fussier than Grandma, who has plastic on all her furniture so it doesn't get dirty. "In case of accidents," Grandma says.

Sometimes I think Waby's crazy. The way she gets mad about stupid stuff. Like vitamins and wearing socks and if my dad doesn't put the newspaper in with the recycling. My mum says, "She's not crazy, she's three." Like that makes it all right.

Mum gulps. It is weird watching your parents when they don't seem to know what to do. But then she gets an idea. She starts picking at the gummy bear's ear with her fingernail. When that doesn't work, she rummages in a drawer for a fork to poke it with. Now I think Mum is crazy. And *she's* not three.

I try shaking her arm. "Earth to Mum! Earth to Mum! I have to get to school!"

"What?"

"I *have* to get to school! I have *art* first thing, and I can't be late for *art*!" My mum knows all about art and me. Our whole school's getting ready for Gallery Night and it's a very big deal. Huge. And I'm working on a very big idea for my piece. I just haven't figured out what it is yet. Big ideas take their own sweet time.

Mum knows all this, but she's in the alternate universe now, orbiting around Waby. She can't hear me because Waby is now on the floor like an upturned bug that can't flip itself over. A boiling-mad red bug. Her legs are kicking, and she is howling so loudly I think Mrs. Peale can probably hear her all the way up at the school office. No wonder she always has my slip ready.

I shake Mum's arm again. "What? Oh! Mimi! Sorry! Yes, school! Go get your jacket! We're good! We're all set!" Actually, I don't think we *are* all set. Waby is crying like one of those little kids you see at the mall at Christmastime who is totally terrified of Santa.

I go get my jacket.

"I give this one five minutes," says Mum, checking her watch. "Okay, maybe ten."

Waby belts out one more really loud, "No red 'tuff!"

She's very smart, my little sister. She is even cute sometimes when she's not terrorizing us. Too bad that is not now.

Anyway, there you have it. It's not even nine o'clock, and already we've had the first spaz of the day.

Like I said. It's a good place to start.

CHAPTER TWO

Now presenting: the Great Miminsky... and sister

I was five when Mum and Dad told me Mum was having a baby. "Can I name it?" I asked Dad. I had lots of good names. If it's a boy I would call it Ernie or Bert or Bustopher or Emmet or Kermit or maybe even Curious George. I figured it would probably be curious. All I knew about babies was that they like to crawl and get into everything, and you have to buy a lot of diapers and hide all the cookies and sit on beanbag chairs for years and years until the baby stops bonking into stuff. At least that's what my best friend Rani's family did when she got a little brother.

"What if it's a girl?" asked my dad.

"Couldn't Kermit be a girl?" Dad shook his head. I tried to think of other nice names.

"How about Gumdrop? Or Peaches? Or Sunbeam?"

I think I wasn't so good with girl names, because Dad just said, "Uh, maybe you should ask your mother."

Mum said kids don't name The Baby. She was going to wait until The Baby was born and then she would know. She said all she had to do was look at me and she knew I was a Mimi.

"Did Dad know too?" I asked.

"Well, your father thought you looked more like a space alien when you were born," said my mum.

"A chubby, purple space alien!" my dad added. "The best little alien ever!"

Mum looked at him like maybe that was enough and he should stop now. She raised her eyebrows at my dad. "But after a couple of weeks he thought you were really cute! Right, Warren? Right?"

"Well, sure!" he said. "You were the perfect Mimi!"

"I know, Mimi," said Mum. "You can pick the nickname instead! That would be special."

I wasn't so sure. Nobody called me anything but Mimi.

"If a nickname is so special, how come I don't have one?"

"Well, you did for a long time," said Mum. "You had lots of nicknames. We called you Mimikins, and Madame Mim, and the Great Miminsky and Doe Ray Mimi. You had so many nicknames ... sometimes we even called you Screamin' Mimi," said Mum.

I didn't remember any of this.

"Screamin' Mimi?"

"Only sometimes, only when you cried. You were always such a *good* little baby." My mum smiled. "And this baby will be just as good," she said, and patted her stomach bump. "This baby will be perfect. I just know it!"

"What happened to them?" I asked.

"What happened to what?"

"My nicknames. What happened to them?"

Mum sighed. "Well, I don't know. After a while they stopped sticking."

I remember feeling kind of disappointed that I didn't have any sticky nicknames. I guess it *is* a job for a kid. My parents obviously didn't do it right for me—I was just plain Mimi. If I was going to pick a nickname for the baby, it was going to be a good and sticky one.

I thought about it all the time in kindergarten while Mum got bigger and bigger. I didn't get any ideas though. Not even when I started Grade 1. Maybe Mum was right. Maybe it *was* better to wait until you saw the baby. Then you'd just know.

So we waited and waited, until one morning Mum woke up and couldn't fit into any of her pants, so she put on my dad's jammies and shuffled around the house clutching things and making funny noises. Grandpa came over and took me to a movie about a couple of cute green ogres and their ogre babies. One of the babies threw up a lot. I still like that movie.

On the way home I asked Grandpa if he had a nickname when he was a kid. "Well, yes, come to think of it, I did," said Grandpa. "My brothers called me Brump."

"Brump? Grandpa, they called you Brump? How come?"

"Short for Brumplestiltskin!" said Grandpa. He started to chuckle. "Later they called me The Brump Man. Or Brumpster. Sir Brumps-a-Lot. Still do, come to think of it."

I thought Brumplestiltskin sounded like a terrible nickname. And Sir Brumps-a-Lot wasn't much better. But Grandpa didn't look like he minded them.

When we got home, Grandma had her coat on. "It's a girl!" she crowed. "Lily June Power!" Then Grandma said something about pounds and ounces and me getting a good sleep tonight because my whole life was going to change in the morning. I was now a big sister. I was now head kid.

At the hospital I got to sit in a big chair, and Dad carefully handed me a bundle of something like laundry, except it had a baby inside. The Baby had a little cap on its head and a really red, puffy face. I didn't think it looked like a Lily June at all. More like a tomato. But Tomato didn't sound like a very good nickname.

It was scary to hold her. As soon as she started crying (which was right away), Dad took her and gave her back to Mum. Everyone said how beautiful she was, and wasn't she just the perfect little Lily? Grandma gave me a new pack of crayons and a doodle book and said maybe I could draw a picture of my new sister. So I drew a squished tomato. Nobody said, "That's very good, Mimi!"

Sometimes it's hard to see what grown-ups see.

Then my dad took out his wallet and knelt down beside me. He took a picture out. There was this baby with the same little cap and red face as my sister's. Except she was not crying, and her eyes were open. My dad turned the picture for

me to read the words on the back:
"Mimi Power, twelve hours old."

"See how much alike you two are," Dad said.

But I didn't see it at all. I did kind of look like a space alien though.

For a while, the only ideas I got for a nickname were Silly Lily, Chili Lily, Lily Vanilli. Nobody liked those. They didn't stick.

Then one day my mum was changing Lily. Lily was crying. I stuck out my finger and she grabbed it and wouldn't let go. She calmed down a little, and I don't know why but I just said, "Baby-waby, don't cry, please don't cry, little Waby." And do you know what? That did it! She stopped crying and turned her face toward me. Her hair was all sweaty and she was hiccuping a bit, but she wasn't crying. So I kept saying it, over and over really softly, and then my mum said, "That's weird. I think she likes it."

Mum cleared her throat and said in a tiny voice, "Baby-waby? Wabykins? Waby?" Lily reached out with her other hand and grabbed my mum's hair. Now she had both of us, tight. Mum said, "Ow!" but she didn't sound like she meant it hurt.

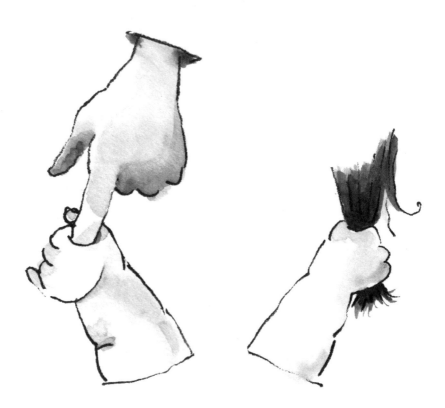

We just stood there, all pulled together, really close.

It was nice.

I think that was the last time I called her Lily. Even my parents mostly call her Waby. They tried some other stuff, like Muffin and Pookie and Lilykins. Once I even heard my dad call her "Pooples" when he was changing her diaper. Good one, Dad. But nothing stuck like Waby.

It's kind of our family secret, the Waby thing. Nobody else seems to think Waby is a cool nickname.

Except for Grandpa.

He understands.

CHAPTER THREE

A do-it-the-self help manual

Waby broke out of her crib for the first time when she was still a baby. I remember because it was my birthday party and she was supposed to be napping. All my friends from Grade 2 were there, and Mum had just cut the cake, when all of a sudden we heard this thump from Waby's room, and then the crying started. Everybody ran to Waby. She was fine, but by the time we got back to the table, the ice cream had melted, and all our slices of cake were floating in pink puddles. Now she has a bed and a little bedroom of her own, and her big ambition is to crawl into my bed in the middle of the night. She gets all comfortable for about a second, and then she starts throwing my pillows and books around, and it's not fun anymore.

Waby fights for freedom every chance she gets. "DO IT THE SELF! THE SELF!" she yells until she gets her own way. She wanted to push her own stroller instead of ride in it (which is when I started being late for school), make her own dinner (usually this means dumping a box of noodles all over the floor) and pop the straw into her own juice box, which doesn't sound so bad except she squeezes the box when she puts in the straw. Everybody knows you don't squeeze a juice box. Waby hates getting juice in the face, but she still keeps doing it.

The one thing my mum likes about Waby's "DO IT THE SELF" is when she helps with the cleaning. Waby is a real clean freak. When she was about two, Mum gave her an old toothbrush and a rag and showed her where the spots were on the kitchen floor. She just went at them and, ever since, all I have to do is give her the cleaning supplies, and I can watch all the Saturday morning cartoons I want without Waby grabbing the remote. Mum is right. "DO IT THE SELF!" can be a good thing.

Waby is crafty in a good way too. She knows my parents can't resist when she begs for something in a cute way, and she says, "an' one for

Mimi too?" The best is when I'm watching TV and Waby brings me a piece of cheese, and I don't even have to get up. Sometimes it's a little warm and mushed up, but it's usually okay. Waby is very trustworthy about this too. She never gets loot and keeps it. She always gives me a share.

I taught her how to say, "Please, oh Glorious Great One?" when she is asking for something. If she asks my mum, she says, "Please, oh Glorious Great Mum?" Even though it sounds like, "PEAS, OH GORY-US GATE UM?" My parents fall for it a lot. They are real softies.

Sometimes she forgets to say please, and Mum says, "What's the magic word?" And Waby goes, "PEAS!" and Mum smiles smugly, hands over whatever it is she wants and says, "Works every time!"

Once though, I said to her, "Except if I ask you for a car."

My mum gave me a crumply smile and shook her head.

"iPad?"

Still with the shaking head.

"Cellphone?"

Again, the *no* thing.

"Pet snake?"

"Oh, Mimi, don't be cheeky," sighed Mum when I'd finished working through my wish list. Waby asked, "Waz chee-key?" And Mum said just never mind and gave her another piece of whatever.

But I am right, I know it, because there are some things Waby asks for that they never give, no matter what. Like the keys to the car, or her own tube of toothpaste (actually, Santa did give Waby her own tube of toothpaste for Christmas, but she just used it to "make spaghetti" on the bathroom floor).

So cute only gets her so far.

Grandma likes to say to Mum, "One day you'll just have to stop twisting yourself into a pretzel for that child."

Grandpa says, "There's no changing people. We have to go with what we've got!"

Grandpa is probably right, and I'm stuck with a cute, crafty, clean-freak sister who can holler loud enough to reach the moon.

Even if she does say "PEAS" nicely, Waby expects super-fast service. If you don't hop to it, she'll yell. Right now she wants an orange Freezie. Dad says, "Fine, go get your mitten." So she heads off to her room to find her Freezie-eating mitten. It's something she came up with herself, because she says Freezies are too cold in her hand. When she comes back she's got her Freezie mitten on one hand and she's ready, but Dad is not moving fast enough.

"I WANNA FEEZEEEEE!" she shouts.

Dad grumbles, "I am not a drive-through, Lily June." But he goes and gets it for her, peas or no peas, which in this case is no peas.

Anyway, it's a good thing we like pickles in our house, because today I brought home bean seeds from school. My teacher, Miss Kwok, gave us each three seeds. We're supposed to plant them in a jar, right at the edge against the glass side. That way we'll see the roots growing.

Waby is confused about the bean seeds.

My dad finishes cleaning out a giant pickle jar and fills it with dirt. I plug two seeds in to show Waby how it's done.

But Waby is crying. "DO IT THE SELF! DO IT THE SELF!"

But it's *my* project. Waby grabs for the jar, so I let her poke the third seed down, and we can see all three of them through the glass. *Perfect!* I try to high-five Waby, but she misses. Like always.

At least she's stopped crying.

Dad does a little motor dance in the kitchen and starts to sing "Gotta make the best of a bad situation." That should be our theme song. The Power family anthem.

Fun for the whole family

Waiting is something Waby doesn't understand. After about a minute of staring at the jar, she asks, "Are they go-ing yet?" (Waby has a hard time with her *R*s. Sometimes she nails them. Sometimes not.) Dad says it might take a week before the roots show.

"Waz woots?" asks Waby.

I try to explain, like we learned in school, that roots push down and help to absorb food and water from the soil so the beans can grow. Which only makes Waby ask again, this time louder, "BUT are they GO-ING YET?"

"Not go-ing, *growing*," I say, shaking my head. "Like Dad says, it takes a week."

"WAZZA WEEK?"

"Seven days. Seven sleeps."

Waby looks like she is thinking about this.

"Naps too?"

"Seven naps and seven sleeps is seven days," I say. "At least for you."

Waby nods fiercely and sucks on her Freezie.
Dad puts the pickle jar on the kitchen windowsill.

"Dad?"

"Yes, Mimi?"

"Maybe I should keep them in my room? They're my project. I'm responsible for them, right?"

I have a skylight in my room. I could put them on the top of my bookshelf right under it. I bet they'd grow fast in a spot like that.

"We can *all* take care of them!" he says. "It'll be fun for the whole family! They'll be fine here. Besides, you know your mum is not too keen on science projects in the bedrooms."

This is true. I had a few episodes involving ink, glue and dirt on my bedroom carpet that even Waby and her trusty toothbrush couldn't get out.

The beans stay in the kitchen.

Seven days does not seem like such a long time to wait. At least not for me. I start counting the days off on the calendar. I make a mark for each day and show Waby. She can count to ten, so I think she sort of gets it.

On Day Four I come home from school, and there is dirt all over the kitchen floor. Waby's arms are covered in dirt up to the elbows, and she has brown smears on the front of her T-shirt. I look over at the kitchen table. The pickle jar is on its side, and there's an avalanche of dirt coming out of it.

"*Noooooooooo!*" I cry. "My beans!"

"It's okay, it's okay, I have them!" says Mum quickly. "She only tried to eat one." Mum opens her palm. The three beans are there. They are a little wrinkled and one has tiny teeth marks on it.

Mum sighs. "Never mind, Mimi. Waby will clean it up." It's true. Waby is actually holding the dustpan while Mum sweeps. But she likes cleaning, so this just makes me madder.

"It's not fair! She wrecks everything! I wanted them in my room. Why doesn't anybody *listen* to me?"

Mum nods and starts in on, "I understand how you feel..."

"Waby! You don't even like beans!" I say. It's true. You should see what she does to Grandma's bean salad. She hides it in stuff. Once we found a mess of it in her Barbie castle. We have no idea how she got it there from the dinner table. "Sah-wee, Mimi," says Waby, trying the cute apology thing.

It won't work with me. I feel like throwing the dirt at her. "Oh whatever!" I say, and stomp out of the kitchen. I try to slam the door to my room, but I left some clothes on the floor and it gets stuck. I flop down on my bed and stare up at the skylight.

The skylight is my favourite part of my room. I remember when my dad put it in. It was after they divided my room in half with a wall so Waby could have her own room. My dad gave me the skylight to make up for it. "Your room might be smaller, so we'll give you a piece of the sky instead," he said. And he was right. I can watch the rain, clouds, stars. When the moon is up, a shaft of silver light pours onto my carpet. It always looks like any minute an alien might appear in the centre of it and start talking to me. Or maybe a leprechaun.

I lie there looking up for a really long time. Maybe a magic beanstalk will appear. The kind you can climb.

CHAPTER FIVE

After the beans are over

Now I'm worried even more about my art project for Gallery Night. After all, if Mother Nature can't create something in our house without it getting messed up by Waby, what chance have I got with art?

Mum said I might feel a whole lot better about Waby if I made a list: Top Ten Great Things about Waby.

"Ten? Ten's a lot."

"Let's not think of it in terms of numbers," says Mum, beaming with pride in her own idea. "Let's just see how many you can think of."

So I think and think, until this is what I come up with:

1. She's cute (but Grandma says she won't be able to get by on her charm forever).

2. She smells like warm bread (most of the time—there are some very bad exceptions).

3. She wipes my toothpaste blobs out of the sink.

4. She is the only one in the family who can find my dad's car keys so we can go places.

5. She gives me all her red stuff. Like cherry jelly beans.

6. She can get Mum to buy us Oreos at the supermarket just by using her cute power.

7. She still believes in magic carpets.

8. She always wakes up happy.

Piece of cake. Mum was right. Sometimes all I have to do is tap into my Mimi Power. Oh, hold on, that was only eight.

Rats.

This is harder than I thought.

CHAPTER SIX

The Kid Whisperer

After Waby was born, my mum started working at home. She asks people questions over the telephone. That's her job. It's called market research. She wears a telephone headset and asks lots of different questions, about the laundry soap people use, or what radio stations they listen to, or their favourite kind of spaghetti sauce. Mostly she works in the afternoons while Waby has a nap and I'm at school. Or at night when Dad is home.

Sometimes Mum gets really busy and forgets to take off her headset. When she picks me up at school, she's still wearing it. With her sunglasses and headset, she looks like a helicopter pilot—a very frazzled helicopter pilot. Mum can be a little absent-minded. That's probably why Waby is always yelling when she wants something. It's to make sure Mum doesn't tune her out. Whenever I see her with that headset still on her head, I make a little V-sign with my fingers behind my head.

That's Mum's cue. She pats her hair, nods like, *Oh, not again!* and takes it off.

At home we're supposed to be really quiet if Mum is working. "Nobody wants to hear a screaming three-year-old on the phone." I wonder if there is ever a good time to hear a screaming three-year-old. Once, Mum was so desperate she grabbed a handful of Smarties and threw them all over the living room carpet. It took Waby and me ages to find them all. After that, Waby was hyped up on candy and wouldn't go to sleep at bedtime. Well, maybe it wasn't just the candy. Sometimes I catch Waby drinking from Mum's coffee cup. She likes to sneak a sip when it's gone cold and Mum's forgotten about it. The day we had to pick up the Smarties, I think both of them had too much coffee. They both stayed up late, dancing around the living room with the stereo on, singing the greatest hits of the '70s.

That was the only time we got Smarties while Mum was working.

Today is Tuesday. We have a new babysitter coming. Her name is Rosie. Mum says she's some kind of Kid Whisperer.

"What's a Kid Whisperer?" I ask.

"I'm not exactly sure myself," says Mum. "Let's just wait and see."

Because of Rosie, last night Mum and I started working on a new list. We have to make a list every time we get a new babysitter. Which is often. The list is all the very important things that anybody who is taking care of Waby should know, otherwise they will have a really terrible time and not come back. Usually they still have a really terrible time and don't come back anyway. But at least, says Mum, with the list it's a fair fight. The list is always changing because there are always new things that make Waby mad, and a few things she has got used to and doesn't shout about anymore.

Together, Mum and I try to think of everything. I write out the new list while Mum washes the dishes. Number one, two and three are easy. They never change.

1. No red stuff.

2. Do not lose Bunny Jim.

3. Tinkerbell is not a doll. Tinkerbell is a flashlight. You will need Tinkerbell to check for trolls under the bed.

4. The tentacles are on the top shelf of the fridge.

5. Two stories, and sing "The Twelve Days of Christmas" at bedtime.

6. Waby always eats standing up. (We don't know why.)

7. No yellow socks.

Waby says all her yellow socks are itchy. Mum saves them, in case one day she changes her mind. She used to say all the pink ones were itchy, and she'd kick and holler and rip them off. Then one day, just like that, the pink ones were fine, and it was the yellow ones that were itchy.

Waby's favourite song right now is "The Twelve Days of Christmas," even though it's nowhere near Christmastime. She has her own words to it: *On the twelve days of Christmas, listen to me... seven days of swimming ... five golden things ... three French toasts...* It doesn't matter if *you* don't get the words right. She yells them her own way.

I write down all Waby's favourite foods for a snack. They are freaky. Most little kids like fishy crackers and cheese cubes. Waby likes octopus tentacles and olives. If she asks for "fishy bits," that means sardines, canned salmon and oysters. She likes cheese, but only the stinky kinds.

Waby is very popular at the deli. The ladies behind the counter think it's funny to give her

weird snacks to try. Squid rings, giant pickles ...
That is where she got octopus for the first time.
Dad taught her to call them tentacles. I'm happy
if someone gives me a breadstick. Octopus is too
chewy.

Rosie, the Kid Whisperer, picks me up from
school. She's pretty and has a soft voice that
sounds like she is singing when she speaks. She
says she's from South Africa. She has kids, but
they're all grown up.

Mum answers the door when we get home.
Waby is standing behind Mum, clinging to her

coat. Waby is also chewing on a mini-octopus, and one oily leg is hanging out of her mouth.

Mum says in a cheery voice, "Thanks for coming. Make yourself at home." Then she peels Waby off and makes a break for the car. Waby starts to holler, and you can see all the little bits of half-chewed-up purple octopus in her mouth. Rosie just gives her a pat on the head. She speaks really softly about how Mummy will come back soon.

Waby keeps hollering, so Rosie crouches down, takes her hand and says very softly, "I can't hear you. You're too loud." She stays there, crouched down, and waits.

Finally Waby closes her mouth. She stares at Rosie, and then she barks loudly, "Wha' cah-lah ah yo' EYES?" Waby asks everyone this. Even though she can see perfectly well.

Rosie just says, "You'll have to speak more softly, I can't hear you."

Waby tries again. *Louder.* "WHA' CAH-LAH AH YO' EYES?"

Rosie keeps holding Waby's hand and shakes her head.

Finally Waby gets it. She whispers: "Wha' cah-lah ah yo' eyes?"

Rosie smiles and says in her soft singsong voice, "Brown. What colour are yours?"

Waby opens her eyes wide and whispers, "Blue, see?"

After that, things go pretty well. We *all* have to whisper, and I forget sometimes, and Waby yells: "You have to WIZZPAH!"

Rosie just waits.

At least I don't have to lock myself in the bathroom to get my homework done. Waby follows

Rosie around the whole time and shows her all her different stuffies, including her all-time and forever favourite Bunny Jim, Keeper-of-the-Peace in the Power household. So long as he's around at bedtime, things usually go pretty smoothly with Waby.

I work at the kitchen table. Tonight I have handwriting practice. I like the loopiness of handwriting. Sometimes I get distracted though, and I turn the loops into flowers or happy faces or hearts. I have filled whole pages with one letter surrounded by art. *M* is a nice letter to decorate. So is *P*. And you can do great things with *L*.

Rosie never reads the list. She doesn't read two books. She doesn't sing "The Twelve Days of Christmas." She doesn't even throw Smarties in the living room. She does find Bunny Jim and Tinkerbell, and she does check for trolls under Waby's bed. But that's about it.

When the sun starts to go down and we get in our jammies and brush our teeth, Waby pulls her usual "Do it the self!" and wrestles the toothbrush out of Rosie's hand. But at least she whispers it. Rosie lets her brush her own teeth. Then Rosie says, "Let's pretend we're on safari." She calls us "bokkies" and whispers stories about South

Africa and upside-down trees, tricky monkeys
and magical diamonds.

We have a great night.

Waby is right back to being loud and "annoising" the next day. I tell Mum and Dad about how to whisper everything, and they try, but then they forget and everybody is back to normal voices. Waby shouts at us, "You have to be PAYSHUNT!"

Then she asks if Rosie is coming back soon.

I sure hope so.

CHAPTER SEVEN

Banana who?

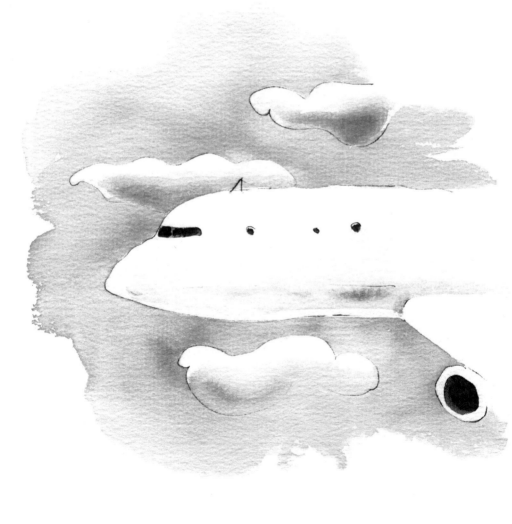

My dad is a location scout for the movies. He drives around looking at houses a lot. Sometimes he takes me with him. I've seen all sorts of houses: giant mansions, log cabins, miniature castles, little cottages with rose gardens. It depends on what kind of movie he's working for. If it's a horror picture, he looks for rickety old houses where the grass is long, the trees are growing onto the porch, the paint is peeling off and everything looks crooked and creepy.

Dad also travels to other places to check out the scenery: forests, mountains and beaches. So we go to the airport a lot, either to drop him off or pick him up. The year Waby was born, Dad came home from a trip. It was on Halloween. Mum thought it would be cute if we went to the airport in our Halloween costumes. I was a witch and Waby got stuffed inside this plush tiger costume so only her face was showing. After that, Mum thought it would be funny if we dressed up every time we picked up Dad, even if it wasn't Halloween. I said I'd do it if Mum did, so that was how I got out of it. Ha!

Mum keeps dressing Waby up though.

This year for Halloween I was a bunch of grapes. Mum blew up all these purple balloons and safety-pinned the tie ends to one of my T-shirts. I had green pants and a little green felt hat. I squeaked a bit when I walked, but I have to admit it was a pretty cool getup—almost good enough for an airport run. I wouldn't be able to ride in the car with it on though, and besides, I really am too old to tear around in an airport in a Halloween costume. Also, I am not so into green clothes any-more. I'm working on getting a whole black wardrobe. Like artists wear. So far, Mum has only agreed to get me black trainers. But I haven't given up yet.

Waby, on the other hand, loves to run around everywhere in her Halloween costume. Sometimes she puts it on at home and plays in it all afternoon. This year she was a banana. It's a one-piece, bright yellow, so you can see her coming from a mile away. And it's all padded and soft, like a great big pillow. Just her face peeks out, and her feet. She looks like a giant stuffie. It cracks me up when she wears it.

For her Halloween trick, I taught her:
Knock, knock!
Who's there?
Banana!
Banana who?
Just Banana!
The joke goes on and on, and you're supposed to answer, "Just Banana!" every time, and then finally when nobody can stand it anymore, you say, "Orange!" as in, "Orange you glad I didn't say banana?"

Waby has to do it her way, of course, which is to forget all about the orange part and just keep saying banana over and over. It's her only knock-knock joke, and she thinks it's great.

Halloween was months ago, and Waby is still tearing around in her banana suit every time we go to the airport. Mum thinks it's a good idea because it gives her extra padding if she throws a tantrum and starts crashing around. Waby is usually good at the airport though. It's just one of those places that really works for her. It's big, and because she's in her padded suit, Mum lets her run around and doesn't worry if she falls down.

I'm always excited when Dad comes home, but today I'm double-so. It was on the news last night that the astronaut Julie Payette will arrive in town today to give a speech. There will be photographers waiting for her at the airport, so Mum says it'll be busy and we have to stick together. I think, what if Julie is on Dad's plane? Wouldn't that be cool? What if Dad asks her to have dinner with us? Maybe we can have tacos, and I can ask her what it's like to see the sun rise over earth sixteen times a day. Or maybe, if it's possible to hear the hollering of a three-year-old from space.

All the way to the airport, Waby practises her banana joke for Dad. I barely hear her though, because I'm talking to Julie Payette in my head. Things look pretty normal when we get there. We see Dad at the luggage carousel before he sees us. We try to run up and surprise him, but it doesn't work so well. Mum has to say "'Scuse me" to a bunch of people, and Dad sees us coming. All of a sudden we are all hugging, and Dad lifts Waby up and gives her a big kiss. He puts her back down, and she does a little happy dance in her banana suit. Dad checks to see if his suitcase is here yet. I ask him if Julie Payette was on his plane, and he says, "Julie who?" but I know he's just kidding. He's cool, my dad. Mum's all excited talking to him too. She's waving her hands like she's doing a puppet show.

Finally the bags start coming down. Waby loves this part. You have to grab on to her, or she will try to climb on and ride around. I know this from experience. I look around for her, but it's pretty crowded. Still, it's hard to miss a three-year-old in a bright yellow banana suit. I take a step back and bump into somebody behind me. Somebody who is not Waby.

"Mum? Dad? Where's Waby?"

Instantly my parents go from happy-puppet-show talking to search-and-rescue mission. All three of us look in different directions. I race around the carousel. Mum starts moving through the crowd, asking if anybody's seen a little girl. She forgets to tell them about the banana suit. This might be helpful information.

Across the terminal there's a crowd forming. For a second I forget all about Waby. I bet it's

Julie! She's here, and she's getting the astro-rock-star treatment. I can see cameras flashing. I can't help it—I know I should be looking for my sister, but I have to see Julie.

"Mum, Dad," I call over my shoulder, "I'm going over here!"

As I get closer to the crowd, I can make out what they're saying. "Oh! Isn't she cute! Just look at that face! Where did she come from?"

Uh oh. That's no astronaut. I see a flash of yellow. It's Waby. I squeeze through some people and get bonked by a couple of cameras before I make it into the centre of the circle. People are waving at Waby and snapping pictures. You would think she would be bawling by now, but instead she's doing her happy dance. A security guard is crouched down, asking her where her family is. Waby just says, "Knock, knock!" and starts laughing.

There are times when Waby is really much more of a ham than a banana.

"Waby! I mean, Lily June!" I say sharply. I'm not sure Waby even knows her real name. "Let's go!"

Of course, Waby says, "No, don' wan' to," and stomps her foot. She's not quite so cute anymore.

The security guard looks at me suspiciously. No one's snapping pictures now.

"Do you know this girl?" the security guard asks. Only he doesn't ask me, he asks Waby.

The truth is, Waby and I don't look like each other, even when she isn't being a banana. She has straight blonde hair and blue eyes. My hair is brown and wavy, and I have brown eyes. My ears stick out a bit, Waby's stick out a lot. I look like Mum. Waby looks like Dad.

"No!" she shouts and crosses her arms.

Just then Mum breaks through the crowd. "Lily June! There you are! Are you okay?" Mum grabs Waby in a big squishy hug. She's lucky she's not a real banana. The security guard raises his eyebrows at Mum. Just then we hear this muffled, "Oops, sorry, excuse me, sorry there, excuse me ..."

Then Dad steps into the circle, and just like that we are all matched up again. It's obvious to everyone we belong to each other. Even if one of us looks like a banana.

CHAPTER EIGHT

Everybody knows ketchup is for squeezing

They have a Great Big Burger at the airport. My parents always take us there after we pick up Dad.

I think Great Big Burger is Mum's favourite restaurant. Waby and I like Happy Face Sushi better, but at Great Big Burger, Mum can load up on ketchup packs and nobody cares. We go through a lot of ketchup packs. Waby loves to squeeze them. Of course, ketchup is "red 'tuff," so she never eats it or wants the packs opened up— she just squeezes them. Dad says Waby is as happy as a clam if she's got a ketchup pack in each fist.

How does he know clams are so happy? Grown-ups have such strange ideas about mollusks. Dad seems to think they make good gifts. He is always bringing back cool mollusk fossils for us from his trips. My mum doesn't get too excited about them, she just says, "Whatever happened to a nice box of chocolates?" but she's

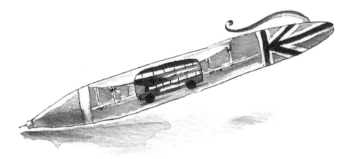

happy that he's home, and she lets him put his "silly rocks" wherever he wants—for about a day.

Until today, the best gift Dad ever brought home was the tippy pen from his trip to London. It's got a red double-decker bus on it that goes past Big Ben and London Bridge. Or some bridge. I don't know exactly which one. It's one of those tippy pens where you tilt it one way and the bus goes down, and then you tilt it the other way and the bus goes backward.

Waby nearly went crazy when she first saw that pen. She thought it was the neatest thing. I did too, and the first chance I got, I hid it. I keep it in the top drawer of my dresser wrapped in a pair of too-small Hello Kitty underwear. Waby can't reach that drawer.

Eventually she forgot all about the pen.

This time though, Dad has topped the tippy pen. He brought home his best gift ever: a prehistoric poo—a chunk of rock, with something that looks like worm squirt on top. "Just think of it!" says Dad. "Millions of years ago some sea worm made its squiggle on a beach, and now, here it is, right in the Power living room!"

Waby looks puzzled. "Woom poo?" she asks in a small voice.

"Well, not exactly poo," says my dad, not wanting to sound too rude. "Technically, it's a worm casting."

"Poo?" asks Waby again, pointing at the fossil.

"Pretty much!" says Dad, jumping straight to the easy way out. Waby wrinkles her forehead and sticks her thumb in her mouth. She got toilet trained by my Dad. He taught her to say "Bye-bye!" and wave at the toilet while flushing.

"Let's just put the nice fossil up here," says Dad. "That way we can show it off when people visit!" He puts his new treasure up on the mantel. He fiddles around, rearranging things, until he's found just the right spot for it.

CHAPTER NINE

There are things even chocolate chips can't make better

I tell Rani about the fossil the next day. Rani and I have been best friends since Grade 1, when we were both late the same day. Mrs. Cubbage, our teacher, sent us down to the office for late slips. She said, "Rani and Mimi, you are a pair!" I looked at Rani and said, "Rani?" and she looked at me and said, "Mimi?" Then we both said, "Nice name!" to each other right at the same time, and we were fast friends forever after.

"Mimi Power, you are so lucky! You get the best stuff! My parents never go anywhere! I would never in a million years get million-year-old anything!"

Rani makes me promise to bring it to school. "What does it look like? What colour is it?"

"Well, I guess it's kind of, I dunno, lumpy and grey."

"Grey. Hmm. Grey," says Rani. "Sounds kind of boring. I know! Maybe you can draw it for Gallery Night. But I still want to see it first, okay?"

I go straight to the mantel when I get home.

The fossil's gone.

Maybe Mum took it for safekeeping. She never keeps anything breakable up there anyway. Mostly it's just stuff like junk mail and pennies and Waby's old sock monkey. It's kind of a scary-looking sock monkey, with a blob of glue where one googly eye used to be, and some unravelling rips on its body. No wonder Waby never plays with it. It looks like it was in a fight with a wolverine and lost.

Anyway, my mum always says the mantel is just an "invitation for d-i-s-a-s-t-e-r," and rolls her eyes and nods over at Waby. Like we don't know who spells disaster in our house.

My parents spell out words a lot. It's their code. Not everything, just important words like "t-e-n-t-a-c-l-e-s" and "t-e-l-e-v-i-s-i-o-n" and basically anything that Waby might want but they aren't offering right then. They also spell out plots against her, like "b-a-t-h-t-i-m-e," when they want to dodge the spaz until the last possible second.

As I head for the place where my parents hide everything—under their bed (I know, what's the point?)—I hear my dad's voice coming from the bathroom. "But where is it, Waby? Be a good girl and tell Daddy ... where's Daddy's fossil?"

When I get to the doorway, I see Waby pointing to the toilet. "Fozzlepoo in toilet! Bye-bye, fozzle-poo!"

Just like Dad taught her. He is very proud of potty training Waby. Mum says he cheated, because he'd promise her chocolate chips if she used the potty, but it worked, so he got the credit.

Bye-bye, Mimi Power, realist fossil painter. I should've known we were never going to see that million-year-old worm squirt again. I think my dad didn't want to believe her. So Waby says it again. She probably thinks she'll get a double dose of chocolate chips. Boy, is she ever wrong.

"Fozzlepoo in toilet! Bye-bye, fozzlepoo!"

I'm not kidding, my dad actually clutches his face for a second and makes this gurgling little "Agghhh!" sound.

"Waby? Did you flush? Did you flush yet?" asks Dad, bending down.

When Waby shakes her head, my dad's whole face lights up. Just like that, he rolls up his right sleeve, thrusts his arm down the toilet and starts splashing around. There's a small clinking sound, and my dad grits his teeth and smiles fiercely. "Almost got it... a bit more... yes... careful now..." He takes a deep breath. "Just a few more inches... here we go... oh... oh... oh...

... *noooooooooooooooooooooooo!*"

We hear the clinking again, but this time it's going away from us. My dad pulls his dripping arm out like it was the losing pole at a fishing derby, and slumps over the toilet bowl.

"Sad Daddy," says Waby, and pats his back with her little hand. Then she chirps, "Bye-bye, fozzlepoo!" and tries reaching for the handle to finish the job. Dad is not quite done though. He pulls Waby back by the T-shirt and says, "Waby, you wait right here. Daddy has another idea. Be a good girl." Then he lowers his voice, which he almost never does except when he really means it, and all of a sudden he's turned into gangster-Dad, saying, "*I mean it, kiddo,* don't move."

Waby nods and sticks her thumb in her mouth.

Right then you would think somebody started a stopwatch. Dad does a mad dash out of the bathroom. He looks funny skidding in his sock feet down the shiny wood floor of the hallway. He slides into my room, which is close to the bathroom, and starts tearing through my closet. "Daaaaaaaad!" I cry, but he just mumbles, "plastic, plastic, plastic," until finally he finds a wire hanger. He grabs it off the pole, yanks my jean jacket off it and starts bending and twisting it like a crocodile hunter wrestling with a boa constrictor. I'm pretty sure he even says "Crikey!" a couple of times. Or maybe something else that I can't say here. Hard to tell because he is huffing and grunting out words that sound a lot like words I know that I am not supposed to know.

Finally he gets the hanger untangled and then retangled the way he wants it. "Stand back, Mimi! This is a job for Super Power!"

I'm not sure what my dad is expecting. Maybe he thinks he might pull up a sea monster or something. He bounds over my bed, takes a flying leap out the door and turns in mid-air to head back down the hall. But when his socks hit the floor, he slips and goes down, the coat hanger boomeranging out of his grasp.

"Yaaaghh!" cries Dad, crashing to the floor.

"Dad! Are you okay?"

He just groans and grabs his soggy arm.

Which is when we hear the toilet flush.

A little while later my dad is lying on the sofa. He is wearing a dry shirt and has an ice pack on his arm and a big pink Dora the Explorer Band-Aid on his forehead.

"I guess we'll laugh about this someday, right, Mimi?" He sighs. "It's kind of funny, don't you think?"

He doesn't look like it's funny. He looks like a dad who just lost his precious million-year-old worm squirt.

"I don't know, Dad. Funny weird or funny ha-ha?"

"Well," says Dad. "I guess a bit of both."

CHAPTER TEN

Just one bite?

In Grade 1, Rani's mum brought her to school by taxi because she doesn't drive, and it was too far from their house to walk. Now that we are in Grade 4, Rani walks to school with her mum. They are still late sometimes because of Chewie. Chewie is Rani's little brother. He is in kindergarten. He doesn't care about vitamin colours, but he never wants to change out of his pyjamas to get ready for school. Sometimes Mrs. Jumani just lets him go in his Spidermans.

Chewie's real name is Sanjay, but everybody calls him Chewie because, Rani told me, he had a biting problem when he was really little. Not people, just things, mostly. Rani said he used to gnaw on table legs, his crib rails, toys. Most of his stuffies are missing an ear or a paw or something.

Now Chewie just eats. He loves to eat. He is not like Waby. He's really quiet most of the time. I think the Jumanis forget about him at dinner. So he just sits there and eats as much as he can until somebody notices that he's cleaned his plate and has his chubby little fist in their rice. This has happened to me when I ate at the Jumani's. So I know.

If I go to Rani's after school, her mother says we have to keep an eye on Chewie, which basically means keeping him out of the fridge. It is hard

work. It's almost as hard as keeping Waby quiet and happy when Rani comes over. So mostly we have to be best friends just at school. Now that we are in Grade 4, we talk on the phone a lot too.

On the phone right now we are making plans for Gallery Night. Rani can't decide what she wants to enter in it. She's got a lot of stuff all ready to choose from: a jungle scene, a watercolour of two polar bear cubs, a sun print she made with leaves and pressed flowers. She even made a collage of Bollywood movie stars from some of her mum's magazines. I think the collage is my favourite. There's even a Picasso-style self-portrait where her face looks kind of twisted and wonky—we both think that it's ugly in a Picasso kind of way.

Our teacher, Miss Kwok, is also the art teacher for our whole school. She's a really good painter and photographer as well as being a teacher. Rani and I agree that so far Miss Kwok is our favourite teacher ever. She asks a lot of questions about our work, and why we did things like we did. And she doesn't always send us for late slips if we are just a minute late.

We need to choose our Gallery Night picture carefully because people are supposed to bid on the art, and that way they buy it and get to take it home. It's a fundraiser for the school, and the class that raises the most money gets a pizza lunch and a visit from ZOOMANIA, which is this really cool group of people who bring in lizards and stuff that you can pet. You can volunteer, and if you are really, really lucky, they will pick you, and the lizard will crawl on your head, and that's cool. They also have a rabbit as big as a Thanksgiving turkey, and a ferret that belly dances.

I like the rabbit, but don't know if I could even lift it. It would take some serious Mimi Power.

Rani is a smart business person. She is trying to think of the picture most people will want, so that it will get a high bid and our class will have a better chance of winning ZOOMANIA.

"Maybe the polar bears. Everybody likes polar bears," she says after a while. "What are you bringing?"

I tell her I haven't decided yet.

I'm starting to get a little worried. "I just don't like any of my stuff this year." I sigh. "None of it turns out the way I think it should."

"Maybe you should just paint and not think so much," says Rani.

She may have a point. I'll have to give that some thought.

CHAPTER ELEVEN

Cake before art

Tonight is Cake Bingo night at school. For Cake Bingo you go with your parents, and every family is supposed to bring a cake. All the cakes get arranged on this long line of tables at the front, and if you win BINGO, you get to choose a cake to take home.

This year the cakes are really fantastic. There's a cake in the shape of a buried-treasure map, an electric guitar cake, a running shoe cake, a purse cake, a teapot cake, a princess castle cake, a caterpillar made out of cupcakes with green icing and red licorice antennae, and even a flying dragon. There are cakes shaped like hats, hamburgers, football helmets; there's even one that's a TV dinner, with marzipan chicken, peas and mashed potatoes.

Mum looks embarrassed when she slips our square vanilla cake with the white icing and rainbow sprinkles next to a statue cake of SpongeBob SquarePants.

Rani's mum didn't even bake a cake. "Well, she did," says Rani, shrugging, "but something happened to it between the oven and the fridge." She points at Chewie.

Rani and I sit together to keep an eye on each other's cards. Chewie is around somewhere, but Waby stayed at home with Rosie. There are lots of numbers called, and people are grumbling because nobody is winning and it is taking too long, when finally somebody calls out, "BINGO!" and jumps up. It's Mrs. Cubbage, my Grade 1 teacher. She goes up to choose her cake, and we are all so jealous watching her. The first one she picks up is a princess doll lying on a twenty-layer cake bed. Every layer is a mattress. The mattresses are all different colours, with icing patterns of diamonds, polka dots and flowers. Poking out from the bottom layer is a green candy pea. Mrs. Cubbage puts it down with a disapproving look on her face, picks up the next one for inspection, frowns, puts it down, picks up the next one and frowns and puts it down, and so on, all the way down the line. Finally she comes to the very last cake on the table. She picks it up. It's an Egyptian pyramid, complete with a gum paste pharaoh standing on brown sugar sand. She marches with it over to the mum who calls the bingo numbers. The bingo mum studies it too, before saying into her microphone, "Ahem! Ladies and gentlemen, boys and girls. Would the person who has taken a *bite* out of *every cake* please stand up? I *think* we would *all* like to meet you!"

Bingo Mum is tricky, because she says all this in a really sweet singsong voice, but we can see she is not happy. That doesn't matter though, because a little kid crawls out from under a tablecloth right in front of our table. He has icing all over his face, and there are finger-streak marks and crumbs all over his T-shirt. His hands are covered in rainbow-coloured sprinkles, which fly all over the place when he waves.

Mrs. Jumani cries out, "Chewie!" and rushes over and grabs him. Chewie just smiles and does a big burp. Rani has to leave early. She gives me her cards, and I promise if I win a cake, we can share it.

Bingo Mum "tsks" into the microphone and tells us we can all just cut out the bitten parts. People groan, but Bingo Mum goes back to calling numbers, and after a while everybody is just glad to be winning cakes, and nobody cares anymore that Chewie got to them all first.

When Bingo Mum calls out "B 11," my right hand shoots into the air. I'm so excited I hold my breath while they check my card. "Yup, folks, we have a BINGO over here! Clear your cards while Miss Mimi Power chooses herself a cake."

I dash for the cake table. There are still a few cool cakes left. There's a red-and-blue hockey sweater and a volcano. The lava looks like beef chili though, so it's actually kind of gross. The treasure map cake is gone. So is the Princess and the Pea. So is SpongeBob. But nobody has taken the dragon cake.

My mum's little square cake is sitting all by itself at one end of the table. Like the other cakes are too good for it or something. I look at Mum, then I look again at the dragon cake. It looks like the end of the tail got the Chewie treatment, but other than that it's really beautiful, with purple-and-orange scales, and wings made out of sugar glass. The dragon's got long false eyelashes and is even holding a marble pearl in the middle of its candy corn teeth. I look at Mum again, and she seems to be very interested in staring at her lap.

When I sit back down beside Mum, they've started the next game. Mum makes a show of studying her cards very hard. "Hey, Mum! Look

what I got!" I hold up the little square cake (well, almost square, except for the missing bite). She makes a mushy *Oh, Mimi* face.

"What? It's my favourite!" I tell her.

"Really?"

"Really."

CHAPTER TWELVE

Art and me

The one thing that's more frustrating than Waby is art. Art and I have a few problems. We have had these problems ever since I was handed a smock and paintbrush at preschool for the first time. Every kid got an easel with a fresh sheet of paper on it. We were told we could paint anything we wanted, anything at all.

I felt like someone had tickled me. I'd never painted before. Mum didn't like messy crafts at home. At least not when I was little. Now she'll give Waby anything, even felts, if it keeps her quiet for a second. Which it does, because Waby loves colouring her fingernails with felt pens. And she's *really* quiet when she does it, probably so that she can get all ten done without getting caught. She's pretty quick. You'd be surprised. Once she even got her socks off and started colouring her toenails black before Mum saw what she was up to.

My first painting was a giant lobster. At least, it's the first one Mum saved. By some miracle, it's still on the mantel, held up by the sock monkey. Red, fiery and with snappy claws—it fills up a couple of sheets of paper. When I look at it, I remember wanting more paper so I could make the lobster bigger. I asked for more paper, and tape to patch it together. I was so excited with my lobster, until Miss Layla, the preschool teacher, came over to my easel.

"What a lovely flower, Mimi! Is it a poppy?"

Flower? Flower? Can't she see it's a lobster? Hello? The red fiery shell? The razor-sharp claws?

I shook my head.

"A rose? It's very pretty. Very!"

"Nuh uh. Nodda rose."

"Oh, it's a rooster. Now why didn't I see that before? Why, I can almost hear it crow."

"No rooster." I sighed. "It's a lobster."

Now if I had been Waby, I would have thrown my paintbrush on the floor at that point and started howling.

"Of course! I see it now! A lobster! That's a beautiful lobster! Beautiful!" And Miss Layla whipped out a shiny gold star sticker, pasted it on my lobster and hurried away.

My parents also learned pretty quickly not to try to guess what I'd painted. They bumbled about for a bit, thinking my first gorilla was a spider, my giant ball of sunshine, a dandelion, and my garter snake, a centipede. It didn't even have any feet! Now they just ask what my painting is. Which is just as bad as not seeing it in the first place.

That's me. I see things in my head so amazing I can't describe what they are. But when I try to paint them, they don't match up. When I was three though, I saw it. I saw the lobster. When I looked inside my mind, that's exactly what looked back at me. And when I looked at my painting, it matched. Now that I'm almost ten, it's different. Nothing matches up. I never see on the paper what I wanted to paint in my mind. It's close sometimes, but it's never quite right.

Except for sky. My sky always looks just right to me. Whether it's on my paper or outside the window. Sky is sky.

I tried to explain this problem to Miss Kwok. She's a good listener when it comes to art problems.

Mum and Dad say everything I paint is great. Miss Kwok told me to get a book about a French painter named Henri Matisse.

"His most famous pictures don't look real, exactly, but there's something about them that's extraordinary. He did things with paper and paint that had never been done before. You need to see for yourself."

So I said I would find a book about him the next time we go to the library, which might be never, thanks to a certain episode starring Waby.

CHAPTER THIRTEEN

Not the smudgy one

They keep little stampers and a stamp pad behind the front desk at the library. All the little kids are crazy for the hand stamps. Mum always makes Waby wait until we've got our books checked out and we're ready to go. That way she behaves, if she knows she's getting a hand stamp.

Usually.

The last time we were at the library went something like this:

"I wanna hand stamp!"

"Waby, you have to say please," said Mum.

"I wanna hand stamp, PEAS!"

Waby stretched up and put her hands flat down on the counter. The librarian put a little ink on the pad and tapped it lightly on Waby's hand. "There you are, dear."

Waby pulled her hand back and looked.

"Not the kicket one! I don' wanna kicket one! I wanna stah! The STAH one!"

My mum's face went redder than the stamp pad. Waby must not be the only fussy little kid the librarian has ever met though, because she just smiled and checked her little box of stampers again.

"Oh my! Well, let me see, here's the star one, right here," and she reached out and stamped Waby's other hand.

This didn't pass inspection either.

"No! Smudged! No smudgy one!"

Now Waby was full-on wailing, right in the library. She was out of hands for stamping and she knew it. Big high screams and tears, then her nose started running, and she wiped her dribbly face with the back of her hand, the one with the cricket on it, and then the cricket got all smudged too.

The librarian stepped back. Mum tried to coax Waby out of the library. But Waby wouldn't move. She just rooted right there on the spot and did her firecracker scream. You could pierce your ears with that cry, Mum always says.

I looked around. Now everyone was staring at us. One guy was plugging his ears. Everybody looked so annoyed. That's when I started wishing for invisible power.

Finally Mum wrangled Waby out the door. The screaming went on until we were halfway across the park, when Waby suddenly stopped.

"Oooh! Dandelion! Pretty!" She pulled up the dandelion with her free hand while Mum hung

on to her with the other. She started waving the dandelion around like nothing had happened. Mum grumbled about how we might be banished from the library forever now. We were outcasts.

Since then, Mum returns our books under the cover of night to the book bin outside. I've had to read all my old *Girl's Own* magazines about a gazillion times, over and over. It's no wonder I'm a little short on inspiration.

CHAPTER FOURTEEN

When in doubt, think like a rock star

Today is Saturday. Saturday afternoon. Nap time for Waby. Everyone's favourite time in our house. It's the only time I can get something finished without my little sister messing with it.

"That's *some sky* there," says my dad, looking over my shoulder and munching on a sandwich while I paint. "Anything going on under that sky?"

So much I can't even say.

"Not yet, just thinking about it."

I like mixing blue and white, not completely, just enough so they streak alongside each other. I can do this for hours. Just blue and white. I never get bored of it. I even like the sound of my paintbrush swooshing across the page. I just want the page to get bigger. Same as I did with the lobster. I wish I had a whole wall to fill.

"Dad?"

"Yes?"

"Do you think it makes sense to like something you're not very good at?"

"Hmmm." Dad munches a bit more on his sandwich. This is his second sandwich of the day. Waby stuffed his first one in an air duct while he was checking his email.

I like how hard my dad thinks about my questions. He always looks like he does most of his thinking for the day while he's chewing. He takes another bite. Finally he wipes his mouth. "Well, sure, I guess. Think of all the rock stars who can't sing."

Sometimes my dad is so smart.

"Working on this for the big show?" he asks.

My dad really likes Gallery Night. So do Grandma and Grandpa. It's all kid art—everybody in the whole school enters something. There are paintings and drawings and collages and pottery. Everybody is supposed to dress up, and the grown-ups drink fizzy juice in fancy glasses and bid on the art they want to buy. Just like in a real gallery. They even have to pay up at the end. It makes lots of money for the school.

You can make whatever you want for the art show. Unless you are in kindergarten. This year, the kindergarten kids are making construction paper penguins with googly eyes. They can do as many penguins as they want, and then they get to choose their favourite for the show. My class is the Big Buddy class for the kindergarten. That's how I know. Once a week we go in and help them with stuff. I'm buddies with this little girl called Amanda. She's very quiet and wears a hearing aid. She doesn't talk much, and if she does, she usually signs with her hands. I am trying to learn sign language, starting with the alphabet. *A* is the easiest. I never forget how to make *A*. Make a fist and you've got it.

Amanda is good at cutting up paper. All the other little kids stick their tongues out of their mouths and grunt when they are using the scissors, and they still rip their paper a lot. Amanda actually makes these tiny construction paper sweaters and jackets for her penguins. Sometimes she cuts out little hats or shoes for them. She always seems happy with how her penguins turn out.

I don't know what this sky is for. I just like painting it. I might put a little pink in, to change the time of day. I don't know what I'm painting for the art show. But I think about it all the time.

CHAPTER FIFTEEN

Waby goes to the dentist

I don't think I have to tell you how this went.

CHAPTER SIXTEEN

Where it goes, or how it ends...

I am tall for a Minnow. Way too tall. Like six years too tall.

All the other Minnows in my swim class are around four years old. Some of them wear floaties on their arms. In other words, they can't swim yet.

Neither can I.

I started taking swimming lessons a long time ago. All I remember is that we stood around in the shallow end every Saturday morning and blew bubbles into the water. I thought that was all there was to it and I was doing fine. Then Waby was born, and I guess my parents forgot to take me to the pool or something.

Now Grandma and Grandpa take me. It was Grandma's idea. She's a swimming teacher. She teaches an aquacise class for senior citizens. It's fun to see her in the pool with the other ladies. They wear swim caps with flowers on them, and mostly tread water and gossip with each other. It looks like they're playing invisible pianos really fast.

Grandpa and I sit on the bleachers and watch them while I wait for my class to start. Grandpa always wears a suit and tie to the pool. He never goes swimming. He just sits and watches us. Even though the air is stuffy and hot and smells like chlorine, he likes it there. He smiles every time I

look at him. While he watches Grandma's class, he hums "Octopus's Garden."

The pool's always busy. At the other end, a water polo team has their practice at the same time as my lesson. They whoop and cheer and whizz the ball so fast it makes you dizzy to watch. It's pretty wild down at the deep end. Grandpa calls them the Tarzans.

My swimming teacher's name is Guy. He has a tattoo running up one arm. I think it's like a jungle vine or seaweed or something. It's very twisty and swirly, but I'm not exactly sure because he wears a T-shirt in the pool, and you can't see where it goes or how it ends.

During the lesson, I always spend a lot of time staring at Guy's tattoo, trying to figure it out. Maybe that's why I can't swim.

Even though Guy is just Guy, he always calls me "Mimi Power." Never just "Mimi." It's sort of funny. The other kids are Tammy and Becky and Caitlin, but me, I'm "Mimi Power." I like Guy for this.

I do not like Guy when he tries to make me float. Then I do not like him at all. He tries every class, and he always promises he won't let go until I'm ready. Which is never. Today I'm still not ready to float. But I know I don't want to be a Minnow for a second more than I have to.

Tammy's a Minnow and she's about the same size as Waby. I slouch, trying to look shorter, when Guy calls us up for the beginning of class. Even Rani is in Dolphins now and gets to go down the waterslide. I need to step up in the food chain. I need to make it at least up to Sardines before Christmas.

So today when Guy calls out, "Bubbletime!" I feel impatient. I don't want to blow any more stupid bubbles. I want to get this floating thing out of the way. Guy hands out the kickboards, and we

paddle around with those for a bit. Finally he starts on floating drills. Tammy goes first. Guy is really concentrating and talking to her softly. The rest of us just hang on to the edge of the pool and watch. Guy takes one hand from under Tammy's back and waves it above his head. Then a couple of seconds later he lifts his other arm out of the water. He's waving both arms above his head like a magician, and Tammy's floating all by herself.

"You're floating! You're doing it! Good job, Tammy. Everyone, look at Tammy!"

All of a sudden I don't know what I am thinking anymore because I am waving my arm and calling, "I'm next! Me! I'm ready!"

I hear Guy call out, "Okay, Mimi Power. Be right with you."

I turn around to see if Grandpa is watching. *This is it. Floating Day. Bye-bye, Minnows! I am ready, really ready. All you have to do is believe... all you have to do is tap into your Mimi Power... all you have to do is...*

BONK!

"Ow!" *Huh? Hey, what was that?*

Guy is right in front of me. I'm still sitting on the edge of the pool, but blinking and trying not to cry. "Mimi? Mimi? Are you okay?"

"What happened?"

"A water polo ball, right on your shoulder!" says Grandma, swimming up.

And I was worried about floating!

"Uh," I say, "I think I'm okay. Nothing seems to hurt or anything."

Guy looks relieved. Grandma takes charge. "I've been bonked before myself. Bit of a shock, but you'll be fine," she says. "Still, we'll call it quits for today, don't you think, George?" says Grandma, looking up at where Grandpa is now, behind me. "How about an early supper instead?"

I remember something about wanting to float. But it's like the spell has been broken. Guy doesn't look like a magician anymore. "See you next week, okay?"

I nod. It's only as I'm dripping my way to the change room with Grandma that I notice he just called me Mimi.

He forgot the Power.

CHAPTER SEVENTEEN

Learning to swim the old-fashioned way

My favourite thing about swimming lessons is the pack of cheesy-poofs Grandpa buys me after my lesson. Usually I share them with Grandpa while we wait for Grandma to finish up with her class. Tonight we skipped snack and went straight to our special restaurant. It's a really nice place, with white tablecloths and Italian food.

I like eating with Grandpa and Grandma. Nobody is there to fling spaghetti or flick sauce. I stay clean all the way through the meal.

"Now, Mimi, this is just a little setback," says Grandpa, closing his menu. "Never surrender! You get right back in that pool next week. Trust me, jump in enough, you'll figure it out."

Grandma raises her eyebrows. "Really, George? Is that how it happens?"

Grandma looks like she is teasing Grandpa.

"Well now, Edie, I don't suppose Mimi wants to hear that old story."

"I do!"

So does Grandma. She gives me the thumbs-up across the table.

"Oh, I don't know, let's see, how did it all start again ..." Grandpa looks dramatically around the restaurant as if he doesn't know where to begin. "Help me out here, Edie, I like the way you tell it best."

This sounds like it's going to be good. I glance at Grandma. Her eyes are sparkling now, and crinkly.

"Alright then, Mimi, but this goes back quite a ways."

"Before Dad?"

"Oh yes, long before your father was born. Before George and I were married, in fact. Your Grandpa, he was quite the fixture at the pool when I first started teaching. All his friends were in their trunks, and jumping in and out of the pool. Not your Grandpa. He always had a jacket and tie and long slacks, no matter how hot it was."

"At some point that summer, your Grandpa started teasing some of the ladies in my class from the edge of the pool. It got harder and harder for me to keep their attention. And Muriel Swanson! Oh, please! Giggling at everything your Grandpa said, like he was some comedian, when he was really a right royal pest!" says

Grandma, not sounding like she minded one bit.

"One afternoon I'd had enough. I called out to him: 'George Power! I'd like to give you a piece of my mind!'"

"Grandma!" I can't imagine Grandma shouting at anyone. Waby definitely doesn't get it from her. "Did anybody hear you?"

"Everybody!" says Grandma, looking pleased with herself. "Well, he really was a pest!"

"I was!" adds Grandpa proudly. "I was an excellent pest! Top drawer! First class! Best pest in show! No topping George Power in the pest department!"

Then Grandpa leans in toward me. "But you see, Mimi, it was all for a good cause. Now, Edie, do you remember what I said next?"

Grandma nods. It's hard to tell, but I think she is blushing. Do Grandmas blush? I guess they do.

"You said ..."

Grandpa doesn't let Grandma finish. He is having too much fun. "I said, 'A piece of your mind? Now that sounds very nice, Edie Sommers, but how about you give it to me over dinner. I'm asking you out on a date!'"

"Grandpa!"

"True! Ha! All true! I felt like king of the pool. Your Grandma, she was speechless. I swung my jacket over my shoulder, said, 'Pick you up at seven?' and was on my way."

Grandma is clapping her hands together and laughing. "And it's been happily ever after ever since!" She reaches over and gives Grandpa's puffy red hand a squeeze with her tiny-bird one. She does not let go.

"But, Grandpa, when did you learn to swim?"

"Didn't!" says Grandpa. "Not a lap! Come to think of it, after that I didn't even hang around the pool anymore. I was afraid Miss Muriel might throw her swim cap at me. Besides, your Grandma never asked me to come back."

"Well," says Grandma, a little sheepishly. "He really was such a pest!"

Grandpa winks at Grandma, and all of a sudden I see a flash of Prince Charming in him. Some of Daddy too. But none of Waby, and she is the only real pest I know.

They are still holding hands and laughing when our lasagna arrives. Just before they go and get all shmoopy on me, I change the subject.

"Grandma, what kind of tattoo do you think Guy has on his arm?"

"You know, I've wondered that myself," says Grandma. "It's really quite amazing, isn't it? A real work of art."

Oh, that reminds me. Art.

• • •

When I get home, Dad and Waby are sitting on the sofa, sniffing perfume samples from one of Mum's magazines.

"How are Grandma and Grandpa?" Dad asks.

I smile and think about this for a second while I pull off my sneakers.

"Interesting," I say, hanging up my jacket. "They are very interesting."

Library, land of disaster

Having a name like Mimi Power makes me wonder, if I were a superhero, what my special thing would be. Most of the time I'm pretty sure I would choose the invisibility thing. That would be handy.

We are in the library. We haven't been here for a while. Not since Waby had her episode over the hand stamp. That was the last time. I usually like it here, if Waby isn't "shaming the family," as my parents say. There's a fish tank at the library, so if you don't feel like looking for a book, you can just stare at the tank and pick out which fish you would like to be if you were a fish. Which seems very appealing to me. Fish are quiet and never scream about getting the wrong stamp on their fin or getting smudgy scales. I wonder if fish even know if they have sisters?

Probably not. They seem so peaceful.

I'm here to look for my missing inspiration. I promised Miss Kwok I'd find that book about Matisse.

Mum whispers to Waby, "Remember, no whining!"

Waby nods.

So I whisper back, "But, Mum, whining is what kids do best!"

Mum gives me an *I-know-that-already* look.

Mum hurries past the front desk with her face down in case the librarian recognizes us, and we go straight for the shelves to see what they have on famous artists. So far, Waby is co-operating nicely. No mention of a stamp. Maybe she's over it.

Mum parks Waby in front of the fish tank, and we go round to the art section. There are lots of books about art.

Mum nervously checks if Waby is okay, and then comes back to me. "Found anything good, Mimi?"

"Not yet," I mumble. The Matisse books are big and heavy. They are all crammed in tight on the shelf. I tug on one but it won't come out. This makes me want it more, so I pull and yank and grunt, and finally it pops out. But I fall back and bump against the other shelf.

"Ow!"

"You okay, Mimi?" says Mum, but she doesn't wait for me to answer. She's already dashing back again to check on Waby. Things are pretty quiet over at the fish tank.

I kneel down and open the book. It's big and has too many words. The sentences are confusing. The pictures are small. Most of them aren't even in colour. Boring.

Mum comes back. "I think we should head out pretty soon, Mimi. Can you hurry up a bit?"

Even when she's being good, Waby is very time limited. I shrug and grab a different book. It's got a picture of a woman wearing a red-and-orange hat on the cover. Good enough.

Mum says it's time to go, and Waby chirps, "Okay, Mummy!" We head for the door. While I check out my book, Waby takes her thumb out of her mouth, puts her hands quietly up on the counter and says, "Star stamp, peas." She even gets her *R* to sound right. The librarian smiles and stamps both of Waby's hands perfectly. Waby checks out her hands, makes a happy grunt and goes back to sucking her thumb.

"Ah, *The Colour Master*," the librarian says to me approvingly. "One of my favourites! Is this for you?" she asks, looking at me.

I nod. I feel kind of proud. I've never picked anything out of the grown-up section before.

"Well, you'll be amazed at what he could do with a pair of scissors. Have a lovely afternoon, ladies!"

Mum beams at the librarian. There are beams all around. We are good girls. Our record is clear, and we are out the door.

Waby trots along holding Mum's hand, and Mum is so happy that she takes us to the bakery for cupcakes.

Waby pops her thumb out of her mouth, barks, "I wanna pink one!" and sticks it back in again. We get four pink cupcakes, and when Mum says we'll save them for after dinner, Waby just nods solemnly and out we go. She's still not spazzy, so we go to the hardware store, fill the car with gas and buy gummy vitamins at the drugstore.

And still Waby is good. This is the best day ever!

At home, we get grilled cheese sandwiches and pickles for lunch. Waby eats everything but the crusts, then Mum takes her to her room for a nap. The house is so quiet, I can finally pull out

The Colour Master for a better look. I wonder what the librarian meant about scissors?

I don't find out then, that's for sure.

All of a sudden the tornado hits. The siren scream. The firecracker wail.

"WHERE'S BUNNEEEEEEEEEEEEEEEEEEEEEE?"

Oh no.

"BUNNY JIM! I WAN' BUNNY JIM! WHERE ... IS ... BUNNEEEEEEEEEEEEEEEEE?"

Bunny Jim did not eat lunch with us. I remember that much. Mum comes rushing out of Waby's room and tears out to the car in her sock feet. I watch her pull everything out of the trunk, yank the seats backward and forward. Bunny Jim is not there. We check the living room, the bathroom, everywhere. No Bunny Jim.

Waby keeps on wailing.

So much for the best day ever.

CHAPTER NINETEEN

Whatever happened to Bunny Jim?

The two most important things in life for Waby are:

1. Her thumb

2. Bunny Jim

Of these two, Bunny Jim is the one we worry about. In our family, at least one person has to know where Bunny Jim is at all times. Usually this person is Waby.

Grandma bought Bunny Jim for Waby before she was born. He was waiting in her cradle for her when she came home from the hospital. Waby has never gone to bed without Bunny Jim.

Never. Not even once.

So much depends on Bunny Jim. Mum doesn't wash him very often. She's afraid the machine will wear him out. So he smells like cheese and looks pretty grubby most of the time. But that's okay with Waby.

We all need Bunny Jim. Otherwise there would be no consoling Waby, ever.

And now he is missing for real. Mum calls Dad on his cellphone. She doesn't have to tell him it's an emergency. She just chokes out, "Bunny Jim is lost!"

I think my dad's super power must be speed, because he's home in a flash. Waby is still crying when he flies in the door.

Dad doesn't even take off his jacket. He grabs some paper and sits down at the table. "Okay, people!" he says. "We're going to solve this like the Super Power Family we are. Mimi, go get me a pen."

I swear my parents had kids just so that they would have more people to find the pens in the house. I can't concentrate on a good search with Waby's squalling, so I head straight for a sure thing: the tippy pen in my dresser drawer.

Mum's eyes are red, and she's sniffling when I get back with the pen. "We'll never find him. He's gone! I knew it would happen one day. I just knew it!"

Mum scurries off to Waby's room with a collection of stuffies and a couple of comforting ketchup packs for Waby to squeeze. This will not do any good. Compared to Bunny Jim, Great Pup, Sheepie and Baboo just don't "cut the mustard," as Grandpa says. But it gives Mum something to do.

"Mimi, it's up to you. You tell me where you girls were today, and I'll draw the map. Then we'll go back and ..."

"Retrace our steps?"

"Exactly," says Dad.

"First we went to the library, then we got cupcakes, then gas, and then we stopped at the drugstore."

Dad starts sketching it out.

"Which gas station?"

I tell him the one that sells doughnuts, and he plots out the map. It looks pretty good. Needs a little colour, but I don't say so.

Dad puts a few quick finishing touches on his gas station, adds a couple of cars, a stack of tires, restrooms ...

That's when I give his arm a little shake. "Dad, maybe we should take a picture of Bunny Jim with us? You know, for identification purposes?"

Dad puts down the pen. "Brilliant!" he says.

I grab a photo of Waby from the fridge. She's in the bathtub with her plastic ponies, and Bunny

Jim is perched on the towel rack waiting for her to get out.

We go to Waby's room, and Dad sticks his head in. "Don't worry, Daddy and Mimi are going to find Bunny Jim. We'll be back soon!" He sounds very cheerful about the whole thing, like it's a good excuse to get out of the house.

I back him up. "Remember, Waby, Daddy's a professional. He can find anything. That's what movie scouts do."

"That's right!" says Dad brightly. "And I've got my trusty sidekick riding shotgun. We'll be back before sundown, partners!"

Waby is not reassured. She scrambles off her bed. "I COME TOO! ME TOO!"

Dad tries to get away. But he's stopped running down the hall in his socks since the fozzlepoo episode. So he is not fast enough, and Waby gets a hold of his pant leg. "I COME TOO, DADDY! I FINE BUNNY! I FINE HIM!"

Dad looks stricken, but Mum thinks it's a great idea. She hustles Waby into her shoes, shoves a box of Kleenex and a couple of ketchup packs at Dad and says, "Good luck!"

Just before we take off, I dash back into the kitchen and grab the tippy pen. There's no time to hide it again, so I stick it in my back pocket. No sense leaving it around for when Waby comes to her senses.

CHAPTER TWENTY

Luck has something to do with it

In the car, Dad looks tense. We go to the drugstore. Waby trots inside and follows Dad up to one of the counters. She turns her big teary eyes up to the clerk, while Dad describes Bunny Jim. Waby is one sad sight. But it doesn't do any good. The clerk just shakes her head. We go to the vitamin aisle, just in case, but there are no stuffed rabbits to be seen.

At the gas station, Dad pulls up right in front of the door. "Stay right here, girls. You can watch me through the window." He jumps out and does this mime of a rabbit while he talks to the guy at the cash register. Then he points to me, and I hold up the picture of Bunny Jim. The guy just shakes his head and starts to ring up doughnuts for a couple of teenagers.

Waby is snuffling loudly when Dad gets back in the car.

"Dad, what if somebody took him?"

Dad considers this. "Well," he says, "let's see. He smells like cheese. He's covered in drool stains, and his stuffing is kind of lumpy. He's not exactly a catch."

I dunno. I see kids sometimes sizing up Bunny Jim. There's something weirdly cute about him. And a stuffie is a stuffie, even if it smells like a wedge of bad brie.

At the bakery, I hold up the picture, and Dad talks to the ladies behind the counter. Waby gets a free cookie and an "I'm sorry, dear."

Nobody gives me a cookie.

"But did you see him?" I ask, as Dad is turning away. "Do you remember my little sister?"

The ladies shake their heads again. It seems nobody remembers Waby unless she is screaming.

We scour the streets outside the bakery. Dad picks up Waby and pats her back. She wipes her slobbery face on his shirt. When he puts her down again, it looks like he's been hugging a slug. Everybody is getting tired and we are almost out of places to look. We head back to the car.

Our last hope is the library. Waby is crying again, so Dad stays in the car outside the front entrance and lets me go in by myself. I give Waby a thumbs-up and run into the library.

Sometimes the head librarian has this sign hanging from the ceiling above her desk. It's there today. The sign says, WHERE'S MY HUMAN? It means there's something in the Stuffie Lost and Found. My heart starts to pound. It's got to be Bunny Jim. It's just got to be! I cross the fingers of both hands. I try not to run, so I speed walk with my crossed fingers. I feel like I need to go to the bathroom, I'm so excited.

It's me! I'm his human! Well, not me, not me exactly, my little sister! She is not quite human, but close enough…

I'm just so sure I see rabbit. And when I get close, I am not wrong. It's a bunny all right.

A girl bunny in a pink tutu.

That slows me down. I shuffle over to the desk and hold up my picture to the librarian. It's a little crumpled. I can't even speak. I still have my fingers crossed. The librarian says she's sorry, but this is the only bunny they've had in all week. I trudge out of the library, and I see Dad's shoulders slump. He knows.

So does Waby. She's crying again before I even get my seatbelt done up.

"WHERE'S BUNNY JIM? I WAN' BUNNEEEEEEE!"

My dad clutches the steering wheel. "I think we'd better go home," he says, sticking the key in the ignition.

From the backseat, the firecracker wailing starts. "NOOOOOOOOOO! FINE BUNNEEEEEEEEE! PEAS, DADDY! PEAS!"

Dad shakes his head, starts the car and turns out of the library parking lot. He turns up the radio and rolls down all the windows. Just as he starts to pick up speed, a garbage truck crosses in front of us, and Dad has to slam on the brakes.

I can't believe my eyes.

"Uh, Dad? Do you see ...?" But Dad can't hear me because of the radio. I think it's Madonna. She's not helping. I poke Dad. Then I point at the truck in front. His jaw drops.

Lashed to the back of the truck, head down, ears flopping, stuffing bulging in all the right places ...

... is Bunny Jim.

CHAPTER TWENTY-ONE

Just your average, everyday, friendly little showdown

Waby sees him too.

"BUNNEEEEEEEEEEEEE!" she screams over the radio. We start waving our arms and yelling, but the truck drives on through the intersection. My dad takes it on the yellow.

"Keep yelling, girls! Yell for Bunny! Yell!"

As we all know, yelling is something Waby is very good at. For sure it's her super power. Dad unrolls all the windows, and I wave my arms in the wind while Waby yells loud enough for all three of us.

But the truck just keeps going with Bunny Jim bobbing up and down, ears flopping every time it hits a speed bump.

Cars try to cut in on us, but my dad sticks like glue right behind the garbage truck. He chases it through more yellow lights, and a red one too. Finally the garbage truck slows down and pulls into a parking lot in front of a dumpster. My dad parks right behind and leaps out.

He calls over his shoulder, "Sit tight, I'll have Bunny Jim in a jiffy! Don't worry, Daddy's a professional."

Waby cheers and claps her hands.

The garbage truck driver gets out and slams the door behind him. He is bigger than my dad. A *lot* bigger. His neck is the same size as his head. He looks angry. "Gonna have to move your car, mister. I gotta job to do here."

"Well, yes! Sure! In just a second—no problem." Dad hitches up his pants and takes a few steps forward, like he's getting ready for a friendly showdown. "That rabbit on your truck is my daughter's."

"Huh?" says the man. "You mean this?" He yanks on Bunny Jim's ear. "Why, that's my new lucky mascot. Sorry mister, he's mine."

"*What?*" says Dad. He's fast gearing up and out of friendly. "Are you kidding? You don't know what I have been through to find that rabbit. It's *my* rabbit."

The man crosses his arms and narrows his eyes. "Finders keepers. That's the way it works, buddy. Now move the car!"

My dad looks like he's having trouble breathing. He bends over at the waist. "Finders keepers?" he says. "Did you just say *finders keepers*?"

"You heard me," says the man. "That's right. Finders keepers. Like it or lump it! Tough beans! Get another rabbit. This one's mine."

Dad balls his hands into fists, and shudders. "Don't make me angry." He stares straight at the garbage man. "You won't like me when I'm angry."

I can't believe my dad said that. I really can't. It's like we're in a page of *The Incredible Hulk*. A bad page. A very bad page. Any minute now, he's going to turn green and burst out of his shirt. I think the garbage man knows it too.

But he's not backing down. For a second though, it looks like Dad might. He comes over to my window and gives us a little update. "Girls, it looks like we have a hostage situation. Which is too bad, because Warren Power does *not* negotiate with rabbitnappers."

Behind us, the garbage man rips the string holding Bunny Jim to the truck. Now he's dangling Bunny Jim by one ear over the dumpster. "You want him? You *really* want this rabbit?"

Dad makes a flying leap at the garbage guy, trying to swipe Bunny Jim out of his hand. It's pretty embarrassing. No wonder we never shoot hoops in the driveway—Dad's so not a basketball star.

Bunny's ear is hanging on to the rest of Jim by a thread. I panic and do the unthinkable. The thing I would not do if I were thinking. I swing my door open and leap out. "Mister, how about a trade?"

I crouch down like a gunslinger and whip the tippy pen out of my back pocket. I hold it out straight, or pretty straight—my arm is kind of shaking. I so don't want to do this.

"A pen? Are you kidding me? This rabbit for a crummy pen?"

See? I was right. A stuffie is a stuffie. Then again, a tippy pen is a tippy pen.

"It's ... it's not *just* a pen. Look." I tip it to one side, then the other. The little red double-decker bus rolls back and forth. At that moment the garbage man's eyes glaze over. I know that look. It's the same look Waby gets when she goes into her pen trance.

I take a step forward and keep the pen tilting from side to side. "Now, please give me the rabbit."

The man swings Bunny Jim back in front of me. Phew, almost there. Once more I say, calmly,

"Rabbit, please."

But he doesn't quite do it.

I tilt the pen to the left. To the left goes the man's head. *Cool.* To the right, and to the right goes the guy's head. *Super cool.* One more step forward, I reach up with the pen, the man reaches out, drops Bunny Jim into my hand and snatches the pen from my grasp. In a flash, Daddy and I are back in our seats. I throw Bunny Jim at Waby, snap on my seatbelt and yell, "Punch it, Daddy!"

Dad hits the gas and peels out of the parking lot in a cloud of dust.

Woo hoo! Home free!

Waby buries her face in Bunny Jim. He looks as tired as the rest of us, but at least he's all in one piece.

"Mimi Houdini!" says Dad proudly. "How's that for a nickname?"

That's when it sinks in. I lost my favourite pen in a desperate trade for a smelly stuffie. And there's a grungy stink coming from Waby's corner of the car. Bunny Jim does not smell like old cheese anymore. He smells like Oscar the Grouch.

My dad and I plug our noses the rest of the way home.

Not Waby though. She's as happy as a clam.

CHAPTER TWENTY-TWO

Just what every girl needs

B unny Jim is now grounded. Dad says the next time he gets out of the house will be if Waby gets married, so he can be best bunny at the wedding. I think this could be a while, because Waby will have to grow up and stop screaming and go by her real name, as nobody is going to want to marry a girl named Waby.

This means Bunny Jim will not be coming dress shopping with us. We have to go because Mum thinks Waby and I need new matching dresses for Gallery Night.

Mum gets really excited about matching dresses. They are hard to find, because stuff for three-year-olds is all ruffly, or puffy, or comes in silly colours or is covered in fairy princess cartoons.

I am happiest in jeans and a T-shirt. I have to keep reminding Mum it's only okay to have rainbow stripes on your jean pockets, or silver shooting stars. No flowers or unicorns, and absolutely no kitty cats. Happy faces are borderline. A few months ago Mum brought home a pair of Winnie-the-Pooh jeans for me. Not for Waby, for me! "They were on sale!" she said. As if that were a good reason for Pooh Bear jeans.

At the mall, there is only one store that has dresses in both our sizes. I like the black ones.

"Black?" says Mum. "For a three-year-old? I don't think so."

"But what about me? I'm not three! Besides, I thought people wore black to art galleries!" I protest. "And turtlenecks—they wear lots of turtlenecks."

Mum seems surprised that I know this. "Well, I can't argue with you on that..." She hesitates. I think I hear a compromise coming. "How about we find a dress with a little black in it? Or a turtle-neck? Something like that?"

"Turdle?" says Waby. She's down on the floor. She found two little cars in the toy basket, and now she's digging for a stuffie. Something to tide her over until she gets back to Bunny Jim. There are no bunnies, but there is a robot missing an eye and an arm. And a Mrs. Potato Head with only her lips and eyeglasses left. Waby gives up and just takes the cars.

"Where is turdle?" Waby starts looking around.

"Not a turdle. A turtleneck," I say. "It comes up your neck like this."

Mum and I start hunting through the racks. Waby starts picking the price-tag stickers off clothes and sticking them on the back of my mum's coat. There are some really nice stretchy velour black dresses. I find one in my size but nothing matching for Waby.

"Mimi, I said no black."

"Can't I just try it on? Please?"

Mum frowns. She has found two matching dresses. They are decorated in ladybugs.

"*Muuuuuuuuuum!*"

"What, Mimi, what is it?"

"Ladybugs are for babies! Can't I please try this one on?" I wave the black stretchy velour one at her.

"Okay," she sighs, "but you have to try the ladybug one on too. Take your sister. I'll find a sales clerk." Mum hurries off. I should probably tell her when she comes back that she has price-tag stickers all over her caboose.

I bend down to where Waby is zooming the cars around on the floor. "Waby, we're going to the fitting room. You have to come, Mum says."

Waby follows me straight to the changing room. I only get my jacket off before she wants to play cars. I forget all about the dresses. Sometimes it's nice to be three again. So we make the cars shoot out from under the changing room door. I send Waby to crawl out to get them, and we start again. She loves it. We are laughing and shooting out the cars. People are going by but nobody stops, and Waby starts shrieking, "I win! I win!" Then she shoots her little car out again, and somebody squeaks, "Ouch!"

Mum swings open the door. A saleslady is rubbing her ankle. It was fun while it lasted. Mum's arms are full of dresses.

"All right, Mimi, time to get started." Mum shoos Waby out with a "Stay where I can see your feet, Missy, I'll be right out." To keep her busy, Mum fishes a new pack of tissues out of her purse, bends down and lets Waby grab them through the space at the bottom of the door. I think there are only about twelve to a pack, so we haven't got much time before she pulls them all out. It looks like she is standing on a cloud. Then Waby starts to get cranky again.

I have to hurry. I try on a pink dress with a poofy skirt.

Mum shakes her head. I agree. Totally. I mean, I look like a helium-filled balloon all set to float away.

Then I try on this weird tube dress.

"Too caterpillar!" says Mum.

The next one looks even weirder: fake leopard-fur trim on a blue jean dress with a kitty face sewn on the front.

All of a sudden Mum says, "Where's Waby?"

"You sent her out, remember?"

Mum knocks her forehead with her hand and rolls her eyes. Then she glances down under the change room door. There are Waby's feet. They are dancing around a bit though, and we hear her grunting. Mum swings the door open, and Waby starts to wail. Except it's kind of muffled because her head is stuck inside the size-three ladybug dress. It's too small for her, and she can't get her arms in or out. She looks like a mad little moth trying to break free of its cocoon.

Mum gasps and tries to calm Waby down. But now Waby is wriggling on the floor. Mum grabs her and tries to find the buttons to let her out, but there aren't any buttons on the dress. There's no zipper either.

"Oh, Wabykins! Don't worry! We'll think of something!"

Mum asks the sales clerk if she has any scissors. The clerk just looks horrified and backs away. Mum tugs at the dress some more. It's no good. The more Waby squirms, the tighter she makes it. Mum tries to pull it up the other way. That's no good either.

She really does look like she's in a cocoon.

A cocoon. Hmmm.

I get down on my hands and knees, and I crawl over to Waby. I'm still in the ugly caterpillar tube dress. "Waby? Waby? Are you a moth? I'm a caterpillar!" I'm not sure she can hear me, so I say it again. "Are you a moth? Do you want to play moth and caterpillar?"

There is nothing Waby likes better than pretending she's some sort of creature. She's always the baby bird or the lamb or the little fish. And I'm the big one. We have never played insect before, but there's always a first time.

Waby wriggles a bit more and somehow stuffs her thumb in her mouth. Now she's quiet and, even better, she's listening.

"Okay, little moth. This is what you have to do to be free. You have to be really calm and still. That's right! Like that!"

There is some snuffling, but Waby is trying really hard to be still.

"Okay, squeeze your wings close together, and stay still, little moth," I say. "You want to be free, don't you?" The dress nods, then stands still again and Mum reaches forward and pulls it up. It kind of peels off, like taking your socks off inside out.

Waby blinks. Her face is red, and her hair is all sweaty and plastered to her head. But she's free.

"Good girl, Waby!" I say, and start to get up.

"No Waby. *Moth!*" she insists, standing up and flapping her arms. "You be catahpillah! You be bug!"

Now that she's free, it's not fun anymore. Waby is back to being bossy. But I do it. I go on hands and knees back to the changing room. Mum says no more trying stuff on. We didn't even get to the stretchy velour. She grabs the last two dresses from the pile. They are yellow and black. "These will have to do, Mimi. Meet me at the checkout!"

At the counter, Waby is flapping her arms and saying, "Me a moth! Me a moth!" Mum is mumbling, "Yes, yes, you're a moth," and signing the receipt. She bought four dresses: the tube thing I am still stuck in, the ladybug dress because Waby slobbered all over it while she was trapped inside, and the matching yellow-and-black dresses.

Mum is grumpy. Maybe this will be the end of matching dresses.

Later that night, when Dad gets home from work, Mum has us try on the yellow-and-black dresses. They fit okay, I guess. When we come out to show Dad, he just laughs. "They look like a pair of bumblebees!"

Waby is thrilled. Mum is thrilled. As far as she's concerned, it's another matching-dresses mission accomplished.

Me? Not so thrilled.

Mum says I don't have to wear the tube dress if I don't want to. We can just take it back. But I think maybe I might after all. With a pair of antennae on my head, it will be a pretty good costume. After all, Waby believed in it. Every good Super Power needs a costume sometimes.

CHAPTER TWENTY-THREE

Power plan

It is now two days before Gallery Night.

I still have no painting.

But I have a plan. I will teach Waby to paint. Actually, that's "teach" with finger-quotes. You know, when your parents don't really mean something exactly the way they are saying it, so they make these bunny ears with their fingers and make them curl up and down while they say the word they are pretending to really mean. So that's my plan: "teach" Waby to paint.

Waby always wants to get in on whatever I am doing, so I think if I get her all set up to paint, she will get bored, go away and stop bugging me. Although half the time when she gets bored, she bugs me more. But this time I have a plan for that too. I have a *distraction*. Mum is always saying, "You have to distract her! You have to be creative!" when Waby is getting pesky. That is not easy though, when the thing she wants most is whatever I have.

I've been trying to collect my own, original distraction kit for a while. Now that the tippy pen is gone (thanks again, Garbage Guy!), the only thing I've got is Dad's car keys, which have a remote alarm button on the chain. Waby loves to look out the window, press the button, and watch the car lights flash and the alarm beep. It only works for a second though, before Mum or Dad comes running. So it's not good when you need time.

Waby wakes up from her nap smelling like bread dough. I ask her if she wants to learn to paint, and she sucks her thumb and stomps over to the kitchen table looking fierce. So much for always waking up happy. I've got it all set up. Water, paints, newspaper over the table ... even sheets of white paper for both of us.

"Let's paint a picture together. What do you want to paint?" I figure once I get her started, I can work on my own.

"House!" barks Waby crabbily.

"Okay, let's paint a house. What kind of house?"

"MY house!" shouts Waby. She pops her thumb back in.

I pick up a brush and go for the blue paint.

"Me do it! ME! DO IT THE SELF!" Waby gets another brush wet and starts mushing it in the paint. This is perfect. Everything is going according to plan. Her face changes and she doesn't look so fierce. She starts doing wobbly lines on the page.

"What about the roof?" I ask her. "Do you want me to do the roof?"

Waby nods. She's still got her thumb in her mouth, and she is painting with the other hand. I quickly paint a black roof above Waby's blue blob house, and then I scoot down the bench to the other end of the table where my *real* painting is waiting. First I need to lighten the blue to just the right shade. Then I'm away ... long strokes on the page, change brushes ... streak some white through ... leave a little room at the bottom just in case this sky needs some land under it. I don't know yet, but I'm painting.

I think, *I'm free. I'm the best big sister ever. Nobody is smarter than me.*

Maybe I'll write a book one day about big sistering ... maybe Waby and I will grow up to be famous sister artists, not the crazy kind who keep a lot of cats.

Oh wow! Look at my sky, this is good, keep going, Mimi!

Waby starts giggling. I love that sound. She has the best giggle. I should make that the Ninth Good Thing About Waby: her giggle.

Then she goes, "That tickles!" and giggles some more.

I look up.

Waby has painted all over her T-shirt. She's painted her arms. She looks like a chubby biker with snake arm tattoos. Now she is mushing the brush into the red. I can't help it. I just sit. I have to see what she does next.

She turns the brush and puts it on her cheek. Then she starts swirling it around.

"Hee hee! Look at me! I FACE PAINT! I DO MAKEUP! Look at me, MIMI! Look at me!"

She's a total mess. I should clean her up before Mum sees her. It's just that it's *so funny*. I start laughing, and I can't stop.

"You ... should ... see ... yourself!" I gasp, laughing and talking at the same time.

Waby pushes down from the chair, runs into the bathroom and stares into the mirror on the door. All of a sudden her glee is gone, and she is freaking out. "I MESSY! I MESSY! CLEAN IT OFF! MIMI! CLEAN ME UP!"

Why can't anything just be fun forever?

A major downside of art is all the cleanup. Even in my book about Matisse, there's this picture where he's sitting in his studio making paper cut-outs. All around him, there are clippings piled up on his floor. And no Waby in sight to sweep them up.

I get a face cloth wet and start to rub the paint off her arms. She looks sort of smudgy. But when I start rubbing her face, the red gets all mixed with the other colours on the face cloth, and she turns purple, then brown and finally grey. She winds up looking like somebody's Eeyore stuffie that got left out in the rain. I don't know how to turn the shower in the bathroom on without getting my clothes all wet.

So instead we go outside to the backyard, where I get the garden hose hooked up to the sprinkler. Waby loves the sprinkler, and it's sunny, so she starts running through. She is having the best time.

This is where Mum finds us. She calls out from the porch, "Isn't it a little early for the sprinkler?"

Waby is shrieking and laughing. The paint has rinsed off and, other than a soaking-wet Waby doing a rain dance in the middle of May, it looks pretty normal, at least for us.

Later, Mum finds the picture on the table. "Uh, Mimi, did you paint this?"

I look at it. "Actually, Waby did that."

Mum's face lights up. "Waby! You're a star! Is it a mushroom? What a mushroom! It's the best mushroom I've ever seen!"

Oh brother. Can't she see it's a house? I mean, I helped with the roof and everything.

Waby doesn't care.

"Uh, Mum. It's our house ..."

"Our house? Oh, of course it is! I knew that." Mum goes on and on about how great the house painting is. She sticks the mushroom/house on the fridge with a magnet, stands back and admires it some more. "Wow, Waby," she says proudly, "I wonder what else you can paint?"

I'll just keep quiet about what Waby really likes to paint: herself. Frankly, parents should know this stuff.

Besides, everybody's happy now, and I've got work to do.

CHAPTER TWENTY-FOUR

The "je ne sais quoi"

This Matisse guy is kind of interesting. He painted pictures with brilliant colours that are so hard to stop looking at. There's one with a lady in a red hat thingy that is very curious. She's not beautiful, but there is something about the picture that makes you want to keep looking at it.

"It's got the *je ne sais quoi*," says my mum when I show her the red-hatted lady in the book.

"The what?"

"The je ne sais quoi. It's French. It means, 'I don't know what.' Sometimes people say it when they mean it has something special about it, but they don't know what it is. Get it?"

I look at the picture again. The woman is still not pretty. But her hat is wonderful. Now I see what Mum means. Je ne sais quoi kind of stops you having to think so hard and wondering what you are looking at. It means you can just look at a picture and like it just because it is.

Mr. Matisse did something else the book calls "painting with scissors." He cut out little figures from coloured paper and made pictures with them. Some are little people. They look very simple and playful. Like marionettes doing the happy dance. There are pictures of circus people, and a boy called Icarus dancing in the stars.

I flip through a pad of Waby's construction paper. Most of the pad looks like a Weed Eater went through it. The only page that Waby hasn't hacked up is grey. It's very blah. It is not a very Matissey sort of colour, I don't think. But I want to work with a fresh page, so this will have to be it.

It is harder than it looks to make something simple. Especially if you are using your little sister's clunky craft scissors. I snip a bit, and then just like that I have my idea. It's like when you are sitting in a quiet room doing your homework and just minding your own business, and all of a sudden you hear the tinkle-bell music of an ice cream truck coming up the street. It's very clear, and you know exactly what it means. Now the grey is perfect. I start cutting these little bendy V shapes. They're too big for what I want, so I have to try a lot before I get really little Vs about the size of the moons under my fingernails. I wreck some while trying to keep the edges smooth, but finally I make five that more or less match.

I take out my sky painting from my folder and put the little Vs on it. I push them around until they are all in the form of one big V. Birds in flight. I try them like this in one corner of the page, then again up in the top right. That's better. They look like they are just about to leave the page. It reminds me of that line in the Mary Poppins song, "Up through the atmosphere, up where the air is clear." So I stick the birds there with a little glue.

Waby waddles dopily into the kitchen. "Wha' choo doing, Mimi?" she asks sleepily, rubbing her eyes.

"Painting with scissors!" I answer happily, pressing down the birds to make sure they stick. "Don't touch it, okay? It has to dry." Waby wanders over to the refrigerator.

I find my thin black felt and carefully write "M. Power" in the bottom corner under the birds. I flip over the picture and scratch *Atmosphere* on the back in pencil, with the date beside it. When I look up, Waby has the fridge door open and is licking the dry stuff off the inside cap of the mustard bottle. I don't know why Mum leaves the condiments where Waby can reach them. Then again, maybe I forgot to tell Mum about her new habit.

Now I feel like when the ice cream truck is leaving your block, and the song trickles away, and everything settles back to the way it was, except that you have a great big ice cream that you didn't have before. I hold up the picture in front of me. I turn it a little one way, then the other.

And for once, finally, I'm happy with what I've made.

CHAPTER TWENTY-FIVE

Minnows and mermaids

"Grandma, what is that?"

"What's what?"

"On your shoulder! What is it?"

"Oh that," says Grandma, waving her hand, "that's my new tattoo!"

"Grandma!" I don't know why, but I am shocked.

"Isn't it pretty?"

It actually is pretty. Which is what you would expect a mermaid to be, sitting on a rock, brushing her hair and smiling.

I gulp. Isn't she supposed to be setting a good example or something? What's next with Grandma? A leather jacket and a motorcycle? I can just see her in a pair of goggles and a helmet, zooming around on a big bike with Grandpa hanging on to her for dear life, his suit jacket and tie flapping in the wind.

"I've always wanted one, so finally I just got up the gumption, and before you know it, I was trying to decide between a sea star and a mermaid."

I'm stumped by this. I never knew Grandmas got tattoos. At least it's not a skull and crossbones. So I swallow and say uncertainly, "Good choice, Grandma."

"Thank you! Lily June thought so too."

"Waby? Waby's seen it?"

"Oh yes, she was with me when I got it done. She helped me choose."

Now I really am choked. Waby was in on it. Grandma sees my face and sort of apologizes. "You were at school, Mimi."

Grudgingly, I can't help but think that the Top Tenth Good Thing about Waby is that she has good taste in tattoos. What if she'd told Grandma to get a Scooby Doo?

We step under the showers to rinse, and I study Grandma's shoulder again. Water splashes on the mermaid, but she doesn't smudge or peel. She just sits there and smiles her pretty smile as the shower rains down. She probably never had to learn to float. She's a mermaid; she was just born knowing.

Grandma shuts the showers off, and we drizzle a path out to the pool. Just before she reaches her ladies, she turns to me and does a mind-reading trick. "You know, Mimi, some of us are born swimmers. I think I was. I can't remember a time when I couldn't swim. And other swimmers have to tap into their ... their ..." Grandma pauses, searching for the right words.

"Uh, their Mimi Power?"

"Exactly!" says Grandma, pulling on her rubber flower cap and tucking in her hair. "Which, I believe, is what *you* were born with. Off you go!"

I head off to sit with Grandpa. We try to spot any other tattoos in Grandma's aquacise class.

"Nope, not a one that I can see," says Grandpa, adjusting his glasses. "Your Grandma is in a league of her own."

When Guy finally calls out, "Minnows!" I am not ready. But I don't want to miss my cheesy-poofs two weeks in a row. This is my great and noble reason for getting in the pool. Despite what Grandma says, I'm still not sure I trust my Mimi Power. After all, when did you ever hear of a superhero who got bonked by a water polo ball and had to slink off to the showers in disgrace?

I am staring down the pool to the other end. I can't take my eyes off that ball. I ignore bubble practice. I don't watch as the other Minnows practise kick-boarding and then float, one by one. The ball stays at the deep end though, and it's whizzing so fast around that watching it makes me dizzy.

"Mimi Power! You're up!" Guy says, and jerks his thumb in the air. I notice that his tattoo is spreading down to his wrist now. It is a pretty cool thing.

Good for Grandma.

"Floatin' time!"

"Huh?" I say, dopily. "Oh, uh, I'll try."

To which Guy makes this Yoda voice and goes, "There is no try, only do," which is very funny, ha ha.

But I almost miss it because I am thinking if I got a tattoo, what would it be? Let's see. Animal? Vegetable? Mineral? Cupcake? And that's when the weirdest thing happens. I push off the bottom of the pool with my feet, and I hear Guy say, "Whoa, just a sec ..." but it's too late. And then it doesn't matter. I'm up. All by myself. And I don't know how it happened.

The next thing I hear is Guy cheering. "Whoo hoo! Mimi Power! Mission accomplished! Mimi Power, you rock!"

Out of the corner of my eye, I see Grandpa come to the edge. "Edie!" he calls, "she's up!"

Hey! It's neat, this floating thing. I could do it all afternoon, I'm sure. I wish my parents and even Waby were here. Instead it gets better than that. Because when I finally drop my feet and find the bottom again, I look up, and there's the whole water polo team down at my end.

"We heard about you, Mimi Power!" says one of the Tarzans. "I'm captain of the team here. Sorry about the ball last week. Glad to see you back."

Then he scoops me up and—*whoosh*—I'm on his shoulders, and he starts jumping, which makes me grab onto his ears.

"Ow!" he yelps. But I guess it doesn't really hurt him because he starts cheering, "Mimi Power! Mimi Power!" and the rest of the crazy Tarzans are jumping around, and the Minnows are clapping and it's just so much fun.

My name sounds good when you are jumping and shouting.

I'm out of breath when Captain Tarzan swings me back down next to the other Minnows. They start climbing on him and the rest of the team, begging for shoulder rides and squealing with the kind of big-time happy that comes so fast out of nowhere that I'm amazed. I couldn't even dream something this good.

I wonder if Mr. Matisse could?

CHAPTER TWENTY-SIX

All over my Atmosphere

Rani is coming with us to Gallery Night. Her parents couldn't get a babysitter, so they are staying home with Chewie. They're afraid he'll eat the whole fruit plate before anybody else has a chance at it. Rani's wearing her sari. Her mum had to do all the folds. It's really tricky, so she only wears it on special occasions. It's shiny gold and flashes when she walks. I'm wearing my black-and-yellow dress. One of us looks like a sparkling firefly, the other like a skinny bumblebee.

Waby has her bumblebee dress on too—with strap-on fairy wings and a tiara from the dress-up box. She gets very excited if she knows we're going out. Bunny Jim is still grounded, so Mum runs around collecting ketchup packs and tissue boxes and fishy crackers to stuff in her purse just in case it's a long night.

Grandma and Grandpa are coming to Gallery Night too. They're all dressed up. Grandma's silver hair is all wavy, and she has on her long pearls, red lipstick and a black dress. Grandpa looks very tall and handsome in his tuxedo. It's hard to imagine anyone ever called him Brumplestiltskin. He doesn't look very Brumple-ish to me.

Dad doesn't have any suits, but at least he's wearing a clean white shirt and his best jeans— the only ones with no holes and no rips. Mum looks beautiful in her shiny green dress and her hair up high. Her earrings sparkle when she twirls for us. She even remembered to take off her headset.

In my bedroom, I am showing Grandma and Grandpa all the art I did this year, except for *Atmosphere*. I am not showing it to anybody yet— even Rani hasn't seen it. It's in my folder. I have to tack it to the wall of the gym tonight before the show. Everybody else has put theirs up already. I'm late, but I'm all set.

My paintings from Grade 4 are all over my bed. They look like friends I haven't seen in a while. There's *Chinese Dragon*, *Tiger in the Long Grass*, *Mouse on a Mountain*.

"Ah!" says Grandma, shuffling through the pile. "Inspired by the famous Jackson Pollack, I see," she says, lifting up a paper with flecks and whip-streaks of paint all over it.

"Actually, I think Waby might have done that one," I admit.

Waby. Where is Waby? And why is the house so quiet? Wasn't she just tearing around a second ago playing bumblebee? But I know that quiet. It's not nap quiet. It's the sound of disaster waiting to happen.

I hop off my bed and check Waby's room. She's not there.

I head for the kitchen. Mum is ahead of me. She freezes in the doorway.

"Jus' UGNORE ME!" I hear Waby shout.

"Don't look, Mimi!" cries Mum as she tries to block me.

"UGNORE ME!" yells Waby again.

I squeeze past Mum and into the kitchen. At first I think it really is no big deal. Waby has pudding on her face and her fingers. And right behind her on the table is a chocolate pudding fingerpainting all over my *Atmosphere*.

I'm crazy-mad! "Waby! You've wrecked it! You wrecked my best picture!"

I just keep shouting, "Wrecked, wrecked, wrecked!"

This is so much bigger than the beans. Gallery Night is ruined. I'm out of it. Our class will never

win ZOOMANIA now, and I'll never get a chance to hug that giant bunny.

Mum goes over to where Waby is waving her arms. She tries to pick her up, but Waby flaps her hands in protest and smears pudding all over the front of Mum's dress.

"Oh!" sighs Mum, looking down at the mess on her dress. "I am so tired of being the napkin!"

Dad, who actually likes getting dirty, sees his chance, dives in, scoops up Waby and heads for the bathroom. So much for his good jeans.

"Mimi, I'm *so* sorry," says Mum. "I know I shouldn't have left her alone with the pudding. I'm calling Rosie. She can watch Waby while we go to the art show."

I don't say anything. I don't say it's okay. It is not okay.

"You know," Mum tries again. "I think we should try wiping it off, maybe there's a chance ..."

"Go ahead," I grumble. "I don't care. I'm not going to stupid Gallery Night. Just forget about me!" I shout and stomp off to my room.

"Wow," says Rani, following me. "Even Chewie wouldn't have done that."

I slump on my bed. "I know."

"He wouldn't have any pudding left to paint with. He would've just eaten it all." She smiles a little and looks at me.

I just cross my arms. I don't smile back. "I would swap Chewie for Waby any day," I say bitterly. "Waby's like living with the Tasmanian devil."

Mum knocks on my door. "Mimi? Can I show you something?"

I stuff my head under my pillow. Rani opens the door for my mum. I hear them say muffled things, and then they both shuffle over to me. Rani gives me a poke.

"Come on, Mimi, take a look."

I lift the pillow and peak out a bit. It's my painting. Mum has wiped off the pudding. Most of it. There are still streaks of brown in a few places.

"Great," I mumble. "Now it just looks like air pollution." I throw it on the floor and turn away from them. Rani picks up the picture and puts it gently on the bed beside me. Then she and Mum tiptoe out of the room.

It's just me and my *Atmosphere* now.

CHAPTER TWENTY-SEVEN

Things that go boing in your head

The truth is, I don't actually want to miss Gallery Night. There's a part of me that still wants to go. I lie on my bed for a long time and imagine flying there through my skylight.

Rosie rings the front doorbell right in the middle of a new hullabaloo. Waby is hollering, "No hair wash! NO WASH!" And Dad shouts right back, "Keep that up, and it'll be a double-soaper!"

Mum yells over him, "Warren! Keep your voice down! And will someone *please* open the door for Rosie! *I have no clothes on!*"

Meanwhile, Grandpa is crashing around in the kitchen and calling for volunteers to come eat some of his famous bacon and eggs. The smell of bacon is coming in under my door.

I hear Rosie down the hall. I can just make it out when she says cheerily, "Now, Power family, we can't all go crazy at once. We have to take turns!"

It must still be Waby's turn because I hear a huge splash followed by a gigantic "Arggh!" from

Dad in the bathroom, and then, "That's it, Missy, DOUBLE-SOAPER!"

After a few minutes more of Waby howling, "NO SOAPER! ME CLEAN!" things settle down, and she starts singing "The Twelve Days of Christmas", like nothing ever happened.

Grandma knocks on my door and asks if I want some supper.

I say, "No, thank you," because no matter how bad I feel, I can't be crabby with Grandma. (I would also like some bacon, but I am too proud to say so right now.)

Grandpa knocks a little while later. "Mimi? May I come in?"

I don't answer.

He opens the door a crack, but he doesn't come in. I see him nodding in the doorway.

"Just wanted to see that you hadn't flown out of the skylight or anything. You never know what might happen when you tap into that Mimi Power of yours."

That is weird that he knows what I'm thinking. Maybe Grandma and Grandpa *both* have ESP. "Grandpa?"

"Yes, Mimi?"

"What do I do now?"

Grandpa doesn't answer right away. "That's a big question, Mimi. I'll think about it and get back to you, okay?"

"I guess."

"Mimi?"

"Yes, Grandpa." I sigh.

"Would you like some bacon?"

I nod.

He quietly closes the door, and a few minutes later he's back with a plate. And Waby. A few octopus tentacles are hanging out of her mouth, her hair is dripping all over her duckie bathrobe and she's holding my art box.

"Just put it down there, Lily June," says Grandpa, sliding a plate of bacon slices over my way. "We don't want to bother Mimi."

Waby puts the art box down, finishes chewing and then says softly, "Sah-wee, Mimi."

Then she goes out the door with Grandpa. Just like that. No fussing or anything. Guess *her* turn at crazy is over.

There's a note on the top of the box. It makes me curious. I get off my bed, go over and unfold it. The message is very short. It's in Grandpa's old-fashioned handwriting. I wish I could make loops the way he and Grandma do.

"One smudge does not spoil a whole sky."

What? What is that supposed to mean? Thanks a lot, Grandpa.

I study my painting one more time. There's really only one smudge on it, and it is pretty small. I wish I could cut it out. I did that once with a dress that I got an ice cream stain on. Mum confiscated my scissors for a month after that. In the end though, she forgot where she hid them, and they're still lost. Six whole years later.

The side window in my bedroom is really old. It's as old as the house—almost a century—Dad says. Wood frames divide the window into six small sections. The glass is all ripply, and when you look through it, stuff on the other side is a little wavy. That's how you know it's really old glass, Dad says—when it looks like water flowing down that was stopped in time. I've looked out this window a thousand times, but have never looked at the actual window before now.

Which is when something goes *boing* in my head.

Maybe my painting isn't wrecked after all. I don't quite know what it is yet, but I have the boing of an idea.

CHAPTER TWENTY-EIGHT

In case of accidents, there's always your Mimi Power

When I finally come out of my room, I have my portfolio in one hand and a few slivers of paper clinging to my bumblebee dress. Mum brushes me off, as if I were Waby after eating crackers.

We sneak out of the house while Rosie and Waby are playing Barbies upstairs. On the doorstep, everybody breathes a big sigh of relief. Things feel back to normal. Dad still has smudgy pudding jeans on, but I don't really mind. That's normal for us too.

"Got something there?" asks Grandpa, looking at my portfolio.

"Yup," I say, smiling at the ground. I don't say any more and Grandpa doesn't ask. He just squeezes my hand and says, "That's my girl!"

At the gym, Rani and I race off to find my wall space. There is a gap between a painting of a moose and one of a Mountie, waiting for me to fit my picture in. I slide the picture out of the folder and stick it to the wall. It's hard to get it straight, so Grandma fusses over it until it's just right, which takes a while.

Then we all take a step back.

"Perfect!" says Grandma.

"Clever!" says Dad.

"Beautiful!" says Mum.

"Better than before!" declares Grandpa, giving me a lumberjack thump on the back.

I can't help myself this time, I think they're *all* right. It is my perfectcleverbeautifulbetterthan-everbefore picture.

Rani comes flitting over to us, as fast as her sari will let her. "That's cool, Mimi. You're a *total* art star!"

I don't have to explain the picture to anyone. I think that's what makes me the happiest. It is six rectangles, each one about the size of a deck of cards. Each one is a piece of the sky I had originally painted. I trimmed the last smudge off, and it's somewhere back on my bedroom floor. There are two rows of three pieces of sky, each separated on the white paper by a plain space as wide as my thumb. Six little windowpanes. After all the trimming, I only managed to save one lone bird from

the flock. It's up in the corner, set in the middle of a clean white cloud.

Miss Kwok comes by.

"Painting with scissors! How very Matisse! And yet so totally original. Mimi, I love what you've brought tonight. I may have to bid on it myself."

Miss Kwok leaves, and I beam at the floor.

Across the gym, Rani looks busy in front of her painting as well. When she comes over for a visit she tells me that most people just want to come up and touch her sari. You don't see little girls in saris very often. They are so complicated. Rani shows me the finger smudges on it, and I tell her, "One smudge doesn't spoil a whole sari!"

Everyone swirls around me, asking questions and making little notes with mini pencils and specially made notepads where they can mark their bids before handing them in at the front table. My little buddy Amanda comes up and gives me a hug. Then she makes signs that the fancy people behind her are her parents. I kind of guessed. Her dad is wearing a tuxedo like Grandpa's, and her mum has a long dress with lots of ruffles, and dangly daisy earrings so big they dance on her shoulders.

"We've heard a lot about you, Miss Mimi Power," says Amanda's dad, reaching out to shake my hand.

I've been standing there with *Atmosphere* for over an hour when I notice a small woman, very old, maybe old enough to be Grandma's grandma, in a wheelchair across the aisle from me. She's talking to a man who looks about Grandpa's age.

The man bends down beside her and listens as she points at my picture. I can't hear what they're saying until some people move out of the way, and the man pushes the woman over to me.

She's so tiny. She's even smaller than me. She speaks very softly, and I can hardly hear her.

The man leans toward me. "Aunt Stella says it's exactly what the view outside her window was when she was about your age."

He sticks out his hand. "My name is Bob," he says, taking my hand and shaking it. "And this is my Aunt Stella."

"I'm Mimi," I say.

"Mimi Power?" asks the man.

For a second I actually feel famous, like he has heard of me or something. But then I see he is looking at my signature in the corner of the painting.

"Aunt Stella is from Big Sky Country. The prairies. Have you been there? She thinks you must've been there."

I say, "No, sorry." But they don't seem to mind. The woman tugs gently on Bob's shirt. He leans down to listen. Then he stands up and tells me, "Aunt Stella says realism is highly overrated. It's always better to paint from the heart."

Aunt Stella smiles, and her hands pluck at the blanket on her knees. Finally she finds her pencil and notebook. I see her start to write my name in the same type of ribbony handwriting Grandma and Grandpa have, only slower and shakier.

There is nothing else written on the page. I can't see what she bid. Maybe it's only like a dollar, but it doesn't matter.

She gives Bob the book and pencil.

He glances at the page. "Whoa, Aunt Stella, are you sure?"

She knits her eyebrows together and nods fiercely at him.

"Just checking. You know your art. Well, I think we'd better go hand this in before you change your mind."

She scowls at him again, and he says quickly, "Just kidding!" as he begins to turn her chair around.

Stella leans as far toward me as she can. Her voice crackles a little, but she manages to say, "Nice dress, Mimi Power."

Bob shakes my hand again. It is all very grown-up.

Then they move away into the crowd and disappear.

CHAPTER TWENTY-NINE

Somewhere back on the bedroom floor

Rosie answers the door when we get home, holding a finger to her lips. We all creep in. The house is very quiet and peaceful. That means Waby is fast asleep.

When I tiptoe into my room, I catch a whiff of freshly baked bread. Through the skylight a shaft of moonlight streams down onto a big lump in the middle of my bed. It's Waby.

I freeze. If I tell Mum and Dad she's here, they'll take her back to her own room, and she'll wake up. Then it won't be peaceful in my room anymore. It'll be just back to noisy normal.

I look around and try to think of what to do. That's when I notice that my room is really tidy. Somebody swept up all the trimmings I clipped to make over my *Atmosphere*. And then I think there is an Eleventh Good Thing About Waby: she thinks it's fun to clean my room. I can sit and read comics, and she will pick up every single thing on the floor and put it in my trunk. If she misses something, all I have to do is point. She is not very good at hanging up my clothes, but she at least throws them in the closet. And she can sort of fold my T-shirts. She's not so good at pants though. They end up getting kind of twisted.

I sneak up to my bed and fold back the covers. With one arm, Waby is clutching Bunny Jim to her chest. Her other arm is flung over her head, and I notice she has something in her hand. I don't know what it is, and I'm too tired to care.

All I can do is try to crawl into bed without waking her up. I don't even change out of my bumblebee dress.

I make it in, but there's just one problem. Waby has the pillow. She's even drooled on it a bit. I can't sleep without a pillow. I lie there and try to think of what to do. Maybe if I just slide it really slowly my way ... *slowly, Mimi ... slowly ...*

Waby wakes up of course. She blinks at me. For a second I think I am going to hear her firecracker wail. But then she just smiles, swings her arm down and smacks me in the face.

"Dis yours, Mimi! I save it! I save it fo' you!"

My little piece of sky. My last little smudgy bit.

"That's okay, Waby. Do you want it? You can keep it. It's yours."

I feel very Big Sister. The sky is a big place after all. I can share a bit.

Waby nods, yawns and wraps both arms around Bunny Jim. I put an arm around her, and I don't let go.

EPILOGUE

They never tell us the name of the person who made the highest bid that night. The school newsletter says, "Congratulations to Miss Kwok's Grade 4 class for earning the most donations!" The newsletter also says it was the best Gallery Night ever, thanks especially to one donor who asked to remain anonymous.

I like to think I met her. I'm pretty sure I did.

I have a new favourite picture in the family album. It's from the day ZOOMANIA came to my class. In the background you can see Rani. She's grinning and holding her hands together in front of her. The ZOOMANIA ferret is belly dancing on her palms.

Most of the picture is me though. Actually that's not quite right. Most of the picture is filled up with Gobble, the giant rabbit. I'm the one holding him up to the camera. You can see me peeking out between Gobble's ears. I'm smiling the same out-of-this-world smile as I did in the pictures of me holding Waby when she was first born.

Waby's in the rabbit picture too. A bit. There's this little pink blob down on the bottom of the photograph. Mum says the blob is one of Waby's fingers from when she was trying to grab the camera.

I think it's okay though. It's a Waby-print. It gives the picture a… what can I say?

A certain je ne sais quoi.

THE END

Matisse and his Masterpiece
by Mimi Power

My picture, *Atmosphere*, was inspired by the work of a real artist, Henri Matisse. He was born in Le Cateau, France, in 1869. As a young man, he studied law but gave up his practice to become an artist when he was in his early twenties.

Matisse became famous for creating paintings with some of the most bold, brilliant colours ever seen. In the late 1930s, when Matisse was in his sixties, he made a discovery—a way of "drawing with scissors"—that he would practise for the rest of his life. He would paint papers with brilliant colours, then cut shapes out of the paper and arrange them into collages to create pictures. With his paper cut-outs, Matisse combined his talents for drawing, painting and sculpture. He cut different figures out of the painted papers: people, mermaids, leaves, flowers, dancers, birds, fish—even circus characters! "The paper cut-out," he explained, "allows me to draw with colour."

In 1941 Matisse needed to have an operation on his intestine. The surgery was serious, and it took Matisse a long time to recover. But he did not stop making art. During his long recovery, he worked from his bed or in a wheelchair.

A young nursing student named Monique Bourgeois helped to take care of him. She also helped him with his art and sometimes painted the paper before Matisse cut it into shapes. Monique liked to paint pictures as well, and Matisse taught her about art.

They became friends. Even after Matisse was better and no longer needed a nurse, Monique would visit him and sometimes model for his paintings and sketches.

In 1943 Monique's life changed forever. She became a nun under the name Sister Jacques-Marie and joined the Dominican convent in the town of Vence, not far from the city of Nice, where Matisse lived.

In 1947 Matisse began a four-year project to design the decoration for the Chapel of Saint-Marie du Rosaire at Vence. Sister Jacques-Marie helped him.

Many years later she remembered how Matisse created the chapel's beautiful stained-glass windows. "For him," she said, "the light was the most important thing."

The chapel took four years to complete. Matisse designed not only the yellow, green and blue stained-glass windows, but also the decoration and furnishings, including the altar cloths, the bronze crucifix, the wall murals and even the priests' robes. The chapel was very important to Matisse. "Despite all its imperfections," he wrote, "I consider it my masterpiece."

Henri Matisse continued to create art until very near the end of his life. In 1952, when he was eighty-three years old, he made his largest paper cut-out, *La Piscine*, on a wall of his apartment in Nice. It's a mural of a swimming pool. Someday I am going to go see that swimming pool. And those windows in Vence too. ★

ACKNOWLEDGEMENTS

At some time in a true artist's life—perhaps as a child— the awareness dawns of the wonderful power of a fine painting and how it can be achieved, in the hands of a talented or insightful person, with mere tubes of colour and a brush.

—PETER EWART, artist 1918-2001

A thousand thanks to the "Book Bandits" of Christianne's Lyceum of Literature and Art in Vancouver: Lily, Kevin, Karen, Cameron, Cole, Nathan, Collett, Aman, Altaf, Mallika, Anita, Peter, Zoe, Jean-Luc, Marie, Neve, Margot, Alex and, of course, Christianne. You're the best friends a Mimi could ever hope to have. Likewise to the Grade 4 students of Queen Mary Elementary in North Vancouver and all the inspiring students and staff in the North Vancouver School District's Artists for Kids program.

Thanks be to Zoe and Aowyn Soane for "eating standing up," a mutual love of finger quotes and sharing the great crib breakout fiasco; Brent Nunuk—the original "Brump"; Dave Jones for kicking it up a notch; Elizabeth Harding for making sure it all had heart; Grandma Marilyn for the swimming lessons; Laura Brock for knowing what it's like; Alison Acheson for the kind of edits that make you happy to take a second look at everything, along with Mike, Carol and the team at Tradewind for bringing Mimi into the light.

Hugs and kisses to Dave and Emily for remembering the greatest "episodes" of the first three years, and to Waby herself... for being real.